"You're not fine."

"Let me go."

"Not until we talk," Matt insisted, as if cozy chats were something they indulged in every day. "You can't keep doing this. *I* can't keep doing it. I thought you understood the hazards I face."

"I do understand." Too well. But understanding and dealing with the danger he put himself in were two different things. The woman he'd first met had been able to handle anything, and he understandably wanted that kick-ass, confident Maggie back.

He wasn't the only one.

Dear Reader,

Watching children grow is a journey of unparalleled wonder. First steps, first day at school, first home run or dance recital, and the list goes on. New adventures are always just around the corner. To authors, characters are like children. Once they escape your imagination and make it safely to paper, they've embarked on journeys that often have minds of their own.

Maggie Rivers has stolen every scene she's been in since *The Unknown Daughter,* in which she bravely faced her mother's illness and fought for her chance to help. In *The Runaway Daughter,* Maggie's best friend begged her to protect her baby boy, and eighteen-year-old Maggie came through, as only a budding heroine could. *But when will Maggie get her own love story?* readers kept demanding.

In *The Perfect Daughter,* Maggie Rivers is now twenty-six and living in New York City. She's an amazing teacher, working with at-risk, inner-city children, and she's found the man of her dreams, NYPD detective Matt Lebretti. Only, the impact of everything Maggie's seen and done since we first met her is finally taking its toll.

Journey with her back to Oakwood, Georgia, while Maggie pieces her life together and catches up with her amazing family. Then hold on tight! More trouble and her very determined Italian detective are following Maggie, too. And neither one is prepared to let her go.

I love to hear from readers. Please let me know what you think of my stories at www.annawrites.com. And join the fun and fabulous giveaways at annadestefano.blogspot.com.

Sincerely,

Anna

The Perfect Daughter

Anna DeStefano

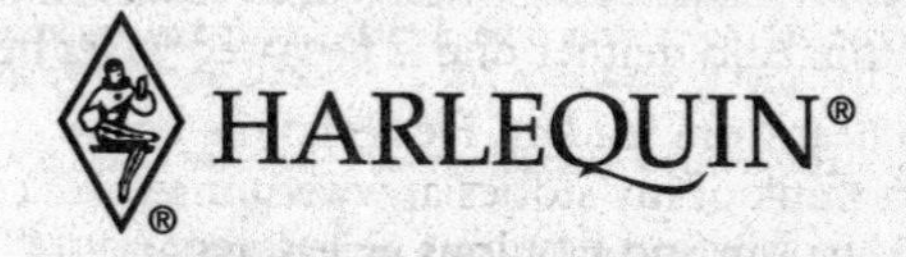

TORONTO • NEW YORK • LONDON
AMSTERDAM • PARIS • SYDNEY • HAMBURG
STOCKHOLM • ATHENS • TOKYO • MILAN • MADRID
PRAGUE • WARSAW • BUDAPEST • AUCKLAND

ISBN-13: 978-0-373-71399-8
ISBN-10: 0-373-71399-1

THE PERFECT DAUGHTER

This edition published by arrangement with Harlequin Books S.A.

www.eHarlequin.com

Printed in U.S.A.

ABOUT THE AUTHOR

Romantic Times BOOKreviews award-winning author Anna DeStefano grew up in small Southern towns very similar to the ones she now writes about. She left home to attend college in Atlanta, Georgia, and soon discovered her very first Italian hero–her husband, Andrew, whom she's been with for over twenty years. When through his New York City family Anna met an honest-to-God hero from the NYC Sheriff's Office, it was only a matter of time before a rugged Italian officer stole the heart of her favorite heroine. So in a way, Anna's been dreaming up the hero for *The Perfect Daughter* since she was a young girl. Next time you hear her say that research is one of her favorite things–believe it!

Books by Anna DeStefano

HARLEQUIN SUPERROMANCE

1234–THE UNKNOWN DAUGHTER
1280–A FAMILY FOR DANIEL
1329–THE RUNAWAY DAUGHTER
1358–THE PRODIGAL'S RETURN

For Lieutenant Thomas Doyle, New York City Sheriff's Office. All errors in this book are mine, but my hero's heart and bravery belong to you and your fellow officers.

You protect what's most precious:
freedom so easily taken for granted.

From the bottom of our hearts, thank you, and God bless you.

And God bless the families who selflessly
share you with a world in which
you're so desperately needed.

CHAPTER ONE

"STOP HOVERING, MOM." Maggie Rivers barely glanced at the woman who'd joined her beside the ornate stained-glass window.

She'd been independent for years. Since she was a teenager, her parents had supported her from a distance while trusting her to make her own choices. But today, Carrinne Wilmington-Rivers was displaying a talent for hovering.

"I'm fine," Maggie insisted. Her entire body was a throbbing migraine waiting to happen. "Please go sit with Dad."

Her father was somewhere in the crowd of Class-A-dressed officers who'd filled the enormous Manhattan cathedral. But her mother had abandoned their perfectly good seats to offer the kind of public support that could only mean disaster. The kind of *lean on me, when you're not strong* display Maggie refused to let NYPD Detective Matt Lebretti see.

Matt and the other pallbearers would be carrying the flag-draped coffin into the church any minute. Then he'd join her near the front. She had a funeral service to get through for a man she barely knew. A man whose death was entirely too personal for both her and Matt. No way was she indulging in a heart-to-heart with her mother. It was already impossible not to picture everyone being there for Matt's funeral, instead of his partner's.

He and Bill had been standing only a few feet from each other when Bill went down.

"I know how hard this must be for you." Her mother squeezed Maggie's shoulder. "If you need anything—"

"I *need* to focus on Matt right now."

Through the cathedral's open doors, she could see him waiting on the steps for the hearse to arrive. Her heart caught at the rigid set of his classic Italian features. He was determined to be okay, too, no matter how responsible he felt for Bill Donovan's death.

"It's not like this is the first funeral I've ever been to." She shrugged off her mother's touch and the echoes of everything she'd fought to leave behind.

"Matt's clearly worried about you." Her mom

blinked at Maggie's wordless glare to *shut up, please.* "Letting people support you while you deal with something like this isn't the end of the world, honey."

Something like this.

A sea of blue.

That's what her dad had said a NYPD funeral would look like. His description hadn't begun to prepare Maggie for the reality.

When she'd started at NYU five years ago, he'd transferred from being the sheriff of small-town Oakwood, Georgia, to a captain's position in one of New York's outlying boroughs. His county-funded job mostly involved enforcing civil laws and warrants, unlike the city officers who dealt with the bulk of the day-to-day violence and street crime. Still, he and his deputies had attended every department funeral since. They all turned out—NYPD, New Jersey police, sheriffs, port authority cops. They showed up in force to honor the ultimate sacrifice an officer could make.

Maggie glanced to where Bill's grieving widow and mother were holding each other in the front pew. Women who'd loved a hero, never believing this could happen. Not really. Not to them.

No one ever did.

"I'll be fine," she assured her mother.

Carrinne walked away in silence. Her expression assured Maggie that she wasn't fooling anyone.

Okay, maybe *fine* wasn't the right word for standing alone in a church teeming with grieving people. But at least she'd earned herself a few moments of silence, free of her family wondering what had been going on since her trip down to Georgia last summer.

Her return to the tiny town of Oakwood for her great-grandfather Oliver's funeral had unearthed memories she'd thought were buried forever. Now, her past had a stranglehold on the life she'd worked so hard for, feeding her fear of losing Matt and her compulsion to run from everything.

Matt smiled solemnly from his post at the door.

It hurt like hell, but she made herself smile back.

"YOU GUYS READY?" Tommy Callihan asked. Word had just come over the radio. The hearse was a couple of blocks away.

"Hell, no," Matt bit out as he turned away from the church.

He wasn't ready for any of it.

It was oddly dark for such a hot, July morning.

Grey-tinged clouds rolled drearily by, threatening rain. Staring at them should have been depressing. Instead, it was a relief.

Anything was better than focusing on the flood of dark blue surrounding him as he waited for the body of his friend to arrive. Or turning around again to find Maggie still watching from inside.

"Oh, my God! I'm so sorry," she'd said three days ago, when he'd told her about the shooting.

She'd clung to him, asking if there was anything she could do, for him or the Donovan family. When he'd left for work the next morning, she'd bravely battled the first tears he'd ever seen in her expressive, brown eyes. Then when he'd come back that night and every night since, she'd clung some more. And he'd let her.

He'd needed Maggie's warm, toned body in his arms, just as much as she'd needed him. Just for a day or two, he'd told himself. Just until he could close his eyes and not see Bill bleeding out while Matt was powerless to do anything but pray for a medical miracle that hadn't come.

But two days had come and gone, then three. And the haunted look in Maggie's eyes hadn't disappeared. A look that was about more than just one dead police officer.

She'd said she was fine. She'd been saying it

for nearly a year, ever since they'd moved in together and things had started to change.

She'd been a force to reckon with when they'd first started dating. Fearless. Magnificent. Then last summer she'd started calling his cell three or four times a day. They'd argued about it, when they never argued, and she'd finally stopped. Next, his long hours and late nights had started to irritate her. This from a woman mired in a grueling schedule of teaching by day, and master's-level courses in education at NYU several nights a week. Then Bill had been killed, and Matt had seen tears in her eyes every time he'd left her since. And that's when he'd finally understood.

Maggie wasn't irritated. She was scared. Spooked by the unrelenting danger he faced as a lead detective on Manhattan's gang task force.

Damn it!

He had a friend to bury. A job to do. A flood of internal red tape drowning him after the shooting.

But what was he spending every waking moment worrying about? Holding on to the woman who'd knocked him on his ass when he'd first caught sight of her at the Central Park softball game she'd come to watch her dad pitch. At twenty-five, she'd been almost too young for him.

But she hadn't seemed the least bit impressed by his bad-boy muscles or the rough-edged charm that most women responded to. Her first irreverent comeback to one of his smoother pickup lines had lured him back for round two. Before the game was over, he'd talked her into going for a beer after, and he hadn't looked at another woman since.

Sun glinted off the windows of the hearse as it turned the corner and crept to a stop at the curb. He, Callihan and the other officers headed down the marble steps, his mind replaying the image of Bill's widow and mother crying at the front of the cathedral, powerless to stop what was happening. Just as they'd been powerless every day Bill had left home to do what he'd sworn to do for the people of this city.

The same job Matt couldn't turn his back on, not even for Maggie. Not even when, more often than not these days, it felt as if he was wasting his time.

There would always be more crime and violence, more too-young gang hoods joining the party, than he'd ever be able to stop. But he did the job better than just about anyone on the force. And that had always been enough. Making whatever difference he could had kept him going, no matter the cost.

Now, the tab included his partner's life. And if Matt didn't do something soon, his relationship with Maggie might join the growing list of casualties.

No, he wasn't ready for any of this.

CHAPTER TWO

MATT'S HANDS caressed Maggie's skin. She swallowed his growl, returning the roughness she'd never wanted with anyone else. Her nails scraped. Her teeth nipped at supple muscles. Their bodies came together one last shuddering time.

Minutes later, their breathing still out of control, he rolled until she was straddling his waist, their chests touching, her brown hair curling madly around her face as she leaned in for another kiss. He palmed her bottom, his fingers long enough to trace downward until she wiggled and collapsed with a purr of contentment. His arms wrapped her in a solid, safe cocoon she never wanted to leave, so she cuddled closer and held on to both the moment and the man that she was fighting so desperately to keep.

"That was amazing." He tucked her head against his shoulder.

Her heart skipped at his lazy sigh, the way it

always did when something felt this right. Then he kissed her temple so tenderly, the impulse to run attacked without warning.

"You're amaz—" he started to say.

"You should go. You're going to be late." She struggled away. Drew the sheet around her as she sat. Wiped at her eyes and cursed under her breath.

Get a grip!

"We have a few more minutes." He curled her back into his arms, then scowled when she shied out of reach. Rolling to his feet, muscles rippling, he yanked on his jeans. "One minute you're dragging me back to bed, Maggie. The next you're shoving me out the door. Make up your mind."

The task force had a lead on the Latino gang members who'd ambushed Matt and Bill two weeks ago. They were tightening the net tonight. Forcing a confrontation that could turn deadly.

And she'd deliberately delayed Matt getting to the station for his midnight call.

"I..." She swallowed instead of finishing, not trusting herself.

I needed to hold you, so I wouldn't think about where you're going...or what could happen....

A masculine sigh yanked her from her thoughts. She looked up in time to see Matt's frown soften.

Why couldn't he have stayed pissed and stormed away, until she was ready to handle him again?

"It's okay to be worried." He crouched beside the bed and took her hand.

Not a good sign.

He was an amazing lover. A tough man with a huge heart to match every other larger-than-life part of him. But tender and understanding gestures weren't his thing. Neither was looking at her as if she might shatter to pieces.

"I'm fine." At least she would be, if she could manage just a little more space between them.

But Matt held fast this time.

"You're not fine."

"Let me go."

"Not until we talk," he insisted, as if delving into inner truths was something they indulged in every day. "You can't keep doing this. *I* can't keep doing it. I thought you understood what I do for a living."

"I do understand." Too well. But understanding and dealing with the danger he put himself in were two different things.

The woman he'd first met had been able to handle anything, and Matt clearly wanted that kick-ass, confident Maggie back.

He wasn't the only one.

"You say, 'I love you,' when I walk out the door—" He sounded almost angry now. Sad, but angry. "—Like you might never get another chance."

"I say I love you because that's how I feel. Since when is that a crime?"

"Since you make it impossible for me to do my job without worrying about how it's going to affect you!" His fists clenched against his thighs. "You've always known what I do. What I am."

"Yes," she agreed simply.

He stood between total strangers and the harm most people never knew surrounded them. But Maggie knew. She'd survived her teenage brush with drugs, and the violence of that world, during the few years she'd lived in Oakwood before college. But her best friend, Claire, hadn't. Maggie's sheriff's-deputy uncle had protected her, but she'd seen with her own eyes the kind of risks officers took. Risks that might one day get Matt killed. And she—

"Maggie?" Matt smoothed a hand through the messy hair that made her look even younger than she was. "It's time to talk about what's bothering you."

"What's bothering me?" Talking like this bothered her.

Everyone wanted to know what was wrong—her parents, the friends she hardly ever saw anymore, the doctor no one knew she'd visited, her professors and her boss at work. But talking, remembering… It only made things worse.

"What about you?" she demanded. "You want to talk? Let's talk about the way you're obsessed with going after that gang that took Bill out, putting yourself more and more in danger with every assignment. It's like you won't quit until you've made up for what happened, even if you have to self-destruct to do it."

Compassion drained from his ice-blue eyes.

"I'm doing my job."

"Is that what you call being on the streets or in the station twenty hours a day since the funeral?" She was working herself up to sounding bitchy, but how else was she supposed to sound, when something precious was dying right before her eyes? "You only come back here to change clothes, grab a shower and maybe fit in a quickie if I'm available. You're not eating. You're not sleeping. Half the time, you look ready to kill someone, or get yourself killed in the process. Why don't we take a few minutes to discuss that?"

"So you'll have even more reason to worry about me and wonder what's going to happen while I'm at work!" He stalked to the tiny closet they shared and dragged on a T-shirt—completing the *uniform* that, along with his longer-than-regulation hair and beard stubble, helped him blend into the inner-city environment he fought so hard to control. "You haven't been able to handle hearing about my cases for months, Maggie. Now you're so messed up about Bill, I've even got your mother asking me to help."

"My mother!"

Maggie's concerned lover was gone when Matt returned to the bed. Calm, unflappable Detective Lebretti gazed down at her now.

"She pulled me aside at Bill's wake. She wanted me to find some way to get you to talk about what's wrong, because she sure as hell can't."

"My mother has no business—"

"She's worried about you. We all are. You're—"

"I'm *tired*." Tired of herself. Tired of everyone worrying. Most of all, she was tired of denying that this broken thing she and Matt had become was entirely her fault. "I'm—"

"You're a wreck, and you won't let anyone help you." The pain in his voice almost sent her back into his arms.

Where you'll only hurt him more.

Disgusted, she headed for the closet, wrapping the sheet around her and wiping her eyes to be certain not a single tear fell. When Matt reached for her arm, she jerked away.

Didn't he get it?

He couldn't help her. No one could—with the screwed-up love she felt for him, or the mess she'd made of graduate school and the summer teaching internship that she was handling as badly as everything else.

The only person who could help was herself, a truth she'd hid from long enough. She came from a family of fearless survivors. It was time she started acting like it.

"Maggie—"

"I… I'm okay." She forced her brain to function as she slipped into the first thing she found to wear. "It's okay."

It felt good, actually, to be pulling her suitcase from the shelf and filling it with whatever she'd need for that night. To be doing something besides delaying the inevitable.

"What…you're leaving?" Matt hovered behind her, his warmth and concern taunting her with dreams that were never going to happen for them. Lord, the man knew how to twist the knife. "I don't want you to leave. For God's sake, don't go tonight. Wait until—"

"Tonight…tomorrow, what's the difference?" They were over. They'd been over for months. She'd simply been too much of a coward to accept it.

The impulse to kiss away his shock sent her back to the closet for more of her things.

When you'd give anything to stick it out for one more night, just so you could hurt your guy all over again tomorrow, it was time to kick yourself to the curb.

"WE GOT 'EM," Callihan said as he loaded the last of their suspects into the back of one of the responding squad cars.

"Not all of them." Matt stalked away, the weight of the night's humidity gluing his shirt to his skin.

They'd cornered six gang members at the crack house. All of them sported variations of the number *13* tattooed on their forearms, branding them members of La Mara Salvatrucha, MS-13—a criminal haven for Latino immigrants nationwide. But none of them had been Luis Flores, the bastard who'd led the ambush two weeks ago.

Luis was going down. Whatever it took, however many basement dives they had to raid, the ex-con belonged to Matt.

Whatever it took.

Including still being there an hour after the raid, instead of back at the apartment talking Maggie into staying.

It was better if she got out now, he kept telling himself. She'd have ended up hating him for what he couldn't walk away from. For caring about her, but not enough to change how he did his job.

It's like you won't quit until you've made up for what happened to Bill, even if you have to self-destruct to do it.

Her warning heckled him as he reached the unmarked car that anyone with half a brain could tell was department-issued. He *had* grown overly possessive of the details of the MS-13 cases, micromanaging when he should have been delegating, haunting the precinct on off-duty hours hoping for a lead and an excuse to head back out on the street.

He dug out his cell phone. Maybe Maggie was still home, packing her things. Maybe she'd calmed down enough to talk.

And maybe you've hurt her enough, Lebretti.

He was no one's idea of a romantic hero. You had to have experienced that kind of all-consuming love before you could give it away to someone else. And the only thing he'd ever felt any kind of attachment to was the job. Certainly not to the emotionless, barely civil grandparents who'd raised him out of obligation. After his coked-out mother OD'd one final time, his grandparents had sprung him from going into the system as an orphan. He'd give them credit for integrity, if little else. They'd fulfilled their responsibility. They'd fed him, beat him when he skipped school, threatened to kick him out the one and only time he'd tried drugs himself.

But love? They hadn't had it in them. Not for him.

Perhaps it was genetic. Not his fault that he'd never been able to give Maggie enough of whatever she needed.

Damn it!

He speed-dialed their number. The machine picked up, and Maggie's funny greeting washed over him, saying that she hoped whoever was calling had a good day.

How was he supposed to do that, now that she was gone?

She'd be with her parents tonight, or with one of her friends. He could find her and try to get her back. Smooth-talk himself into another few days. A week or two. But Maggie clearly wanted out.

Finally, he had the power to give her exactly what she needed.

CHAPTER THREE

THERE STILL WASN'T much to say about the Oakwood, Georgia, airport. There wasn't much to it, period.

Maggie would never forget following her New York through-and-through mother down here ten years ago, only to discover that this *nowhere* place had actually been her mom's childhood home.

Pulling her suitcase behind her, juggling the overflowing shopping bags full of gifts she carried in the other hand, she made for the tiny building that served as the terminal. The heat from the afternoon sun wafted up from the blacktop. Katydids chirped their hypnotic rhythm. At sixteen, her first impression had been that life in Oakwood was as backward as things got.

She'd had no way of knowing how much this place or the people living here would come to mean to her. Or how vital returning would become, though the decision had been more of an impulse at first. A way out. A chance for a little peace from everything and everyone she'd left in Manhattan.

She caught sight of the gorgeous man waiting for her just inside and felt everything slip away as the grin spread across her face. Waving through the grimy glass separating the tarmac from the airport's waiting area, she jogged the final few feet to the door.

"Mom said you probably wouldn't be here!" She threw herself into her uncle's arms and squealed as he twirled her around.

The handful of other passengers who'd de-planed edged around their Kodak moment.

"It's the middle of the day." She gave Tony's shoulder a playful punch. "I could have taken a cab to the house."

She'd actually been counting on a little more time to herself, before having to deal with the family.

"I took off from the station early. Had to grab my chance to have you all to myself." He tweaked her nose.

The big-brotherly gesture earned him another hug. Only seven years her senior and looking so much like her and her dad it was spooky sometimes, *big brother* had always suited Tony better than *uncle.* And after everything they'd been through with Claire, they'd grown as close as any siblings could.

"You're such a big deal around town now." She busied herself with the bags she'd dropped. "I feel guilty tearing you away like this."

He'd once broken hearts all over the county. That was until Tony had fallen head over heels for Oakwood's then-chief deputy, Angie Carter. Since then, they'd adopted two children and twice as many pets of varying pedigrees, filling the old house Tony and her dad had grown up in with the noise and laughter and love it had been built for.

"Never too tired for family, Maggs." He grabbed her things, shrugging off her attempt to reclaim them. Eyes as dark as her own shifted from warm to worried so fast there was no time to brace herself. "This will always be your home, whenever you need it."

So her mother had told all. What little the woman knew, anyway.

"How're you liking being chief?" She inched away, steering clear of the questions swimming in her uncle's eyes.

He'd been promoted since she'd last been home. His sheriff wife hadn't run for another term, opting for an extended leave of absence that coincided with the adoption of newborn Sarah. Tony had been paying his dues as a deputy in the nearby town of Pineview, avoiding the conflict of interest working in the same department as his wife would have caused. The arrival of Oakwood's new sheriff had been the perfect opportunity for him to transfer back closer to home, and it hadn't taken Sam Lewis long to see Tony's potential. With no one else interested in volleying for the chief's spot, Tony had been a slam dunk.

"It's busy as hell." He led the way to the parking area out front. "Annoyingly administrative a lot of the time. But there's plenty going on. The local gangs are making even more trouble than usual. We're looking to partner with the Pineview sheriff to put the brakes on the violence between their roughest gang and ours."

Her only reply was to roll her eyes.

"Isn't that the kind of stuff Matt works on?" he asked. "Some gang suppression unit?"

Subtlety had never been Tony's forte.

The question earned him a barely audible, "Yep," as they reached the beaten-up truck he'd offered to let her use while she was in town.

She'd come to Oakwood to move on. To yank her head out of her ass and pull her life together.

Chatting about her ex wasn't how she'd intended to kick things off.

He opened the passenger door for her. Once she'd climbed in, he stored her things in the back of the cab and walked around the truck to slide behind the wheel.

"There are kids and pets climbing the walls at home waiting for you." He fired up the ancient but perfectly tuned engine. "You have no idea what you're getting yourself into. Lissa and her girls are there for dinner. They haven't decided if they're sleeping over or not. You'll be lucky if you don't end up with a trio of munchkins in your bed tonight."

"How is Lissa?" Angie's recently divorced sister was just the kind of landmine-free topic Maggie needed.

"She's making things work," Tony grunted. "Kicking Chris out was the right thing to do. I can't believe the jerk was steppin' out on her for over a year. I think having the divorce behind her helps. But it's hard, you know? She's always been so together and had everything figured out. Angie's worried she's blaming herself for not seeing it coming, and that's just bullshit."

"I think she's amazing." Any woman who'd found out that her husband was about to have a baby with his secretary deserved to curl up in a corner somewhere and cry for the next couple of years. But not Angie's sister. Sweet, gentle Lissa Carter had come out swinging, grabbing the fastest uncontested divorce in Oakwood history and insisting on full custody of her adorable little girls. Then she'd taken her dusty finance degree out for a spin and landed herself a full-time job at the bank. "I'm glad I could get away for the rest of the summer and help watch the kids while she sorts things out."

They left the tiny airport behind, the Chevy's wheels spraying up a cloud of gravel and clay. Several minutes of blessed silence passed. Then came Tony's long, sideways glance.

Too bad fifteen-year-old trucks didn't come with a convenient escape hatch.

"I thought you were spending the summer finishing the internship for your master's," he said. "Some inner-city program that fits with your thesis on teaching in high-risk environments."

At a city school smack-dab in the middle of the precinct Matt's task force patrolled nearly every day? Headed by the administrator who'd insisted she seek professional counseling, or she needn't show up for work again?

Oh yeah, she'd almost forgotten!

"There's no rush," she hedged. Actually, there might be no degree if she didn't get her act together. "I can finish the teaching requirements any time between now and when I defend my thesis."

Her studies in her chosen specialty, helping special-needs kids in underfunded schools, had veered off track as completely as everything else in New York had over the last year. The unpredictable, everyday challenges she'd always craved had become hurdles she found harder and harder to clear.

"You finish your degree next spring, right?"

"So?"

"So, Carrinne mentioned you've got two semesters of course work to cram in between then and now," said the man who'd felt so strongly about collegiate pursuits that he'd opted for the police academy over freshman English.

"So!"

"So, as much as Angie's relieved her sister has the help we can't give her now that we have the new baby, no one's feeling very good about you messing up your plans for graduation. Unless there's some other reason you're hiding out down here."

"Back off, Tony." She winced at the whine in her voice. "I didn't need this from my parents before I left, and I don't need it from you now."

He whistled softly, returning his attention to the farmland rolling by. The truck jolted over a particularly enthusiastic pothole, giving the creaky shocks something to think about. The sweet smell of freshly cut hay scented the breeze rushing in through their open windows—south Georgia air-conditioning, Tony had once called it.

"That boy of yours must have screwed up big-time," he muttered. "This is the first time I've seen you run from anything."

If only the problem were as simple as how badly *she'd* screwed things up with Matt.

"I'm not running. I'm here to take care of Oliver's estate." A mansion and an invested fortune molding away in a trust, waiting for her to decide which charities to give it away to. She hadn't had a second to deal with any of it since learning she'd been named executor instead of her mother. Now, the responsibility had become her ticket out of New York, a healthy diversion until she could pull herself together and get back to her life. "Once I finish my degree, it could be a long time before I make it back down here. I missed everyone, so I'm hanging out for a while instead of a couple of long weekends. What's the big deal with taking a little time off?"

"No big deal. I figure if anyone's due some

R and R, it's you." Tony flashed the grin that had always been more charming than should be legal. "I just wanted to get the uncle-niece chit-chat out of the way. I promised your mama I'd pump you for info. All that responsibility hanging over my head would have ruined the spaghetti dinner Angie's got simmering on the stove."

He'd been baiting her. Getting a feel for how upset she really was.

Well, now he knew.

And, damn it if the thought of swallowing spicy pasta and smiling for the family she'd been so eager to see didn't suddenly seem impossible. If she begged Tony to drive around for a few more hours, he probably would. They could come up with an excuse for missing supper. But then she'd be running again, just like he'd said. And that's not what she'd come back to Oakwood to do. What she'd left Matt to do.

She could handle tonight and her family's misguided hovering. She could handle letting Matt go, even though she felt him inside her still, with each beat of her heart. And by the time she headed back to New York, she'd be ready to handle everything else that waited for her there.

One step at a time, kiddo.

You can do this.

She forced herself to breathe as the truck seemed to shrink around them. Forced her fingers to loosen their death grip on the door handle.

"YOU REALLY THINK she's come all the way down here just to deal with Wilmington's trust fund and babysit Callie and Meagan?" Lissa Carter was helping her sister wage war on the remains of the evening's celebratory spaghetti dinner. Or, *sge-phetti,* as four-year-old Garret called it.

Angie and Tony's oldest had dumped half his pasta in his lap during the course of the meal, after he'd tested the viability of turning his noodles and red sauce into shampoo. But his parents had barely noticed. After years of scrimping and saving, waiting for the endless paperwork to be processed, then worrying about the countless things that could have gone wrong as they adopted their two Russian angels, Lissa's sister and brother-in-law weren't the kind of parents to cringe at collateral spaghetti damage. Add Maggie's homecoming to the mix, and Garret could have finger-painted the walls with sauce and no one would have cared.

"I think breaking up with that detective of hers helped make her mind up to finally take care of things down here." As at home in the role of house-wife as she'd been as Oakwood's sheriff, Angie scoured the cast-iron frying pan with the same attention to detail she applied to every other part of her life. "They'd been living together for over a year. Things were pretty serious, according to Carrinne. But Maggie seems to be handling it okay."

"How okay is it to want to live by herself at her great-grandfather's moldy mansion, instead of using her old room here?"

Maggie had announced her plans not to stay at the Rivers house over garlic bread and her second glass of merlot. Some nonsense about it being easier to work with Oliver's accountants and lawyer at the mansion, and not wanting to interrupt Angie and Tony's schedules as she helped Lissa with the girls.

"She's just trying to be considerate," Angie reasoned.

"She was scouting for the nearest exit."

"What are you saying?" Angie turned off the water she'd been using to rinse.

"I was okay, too, remember?" Lissa grabbed the frying pan and a dish towel and began to dry. "Everything was perfect for a long time, just the way Mom and Dad wanted our lives to be, even though I knew better." Being fine had been her duty to her parents from the cradle. "I got so good at being okay, it took me months to admit to anyone that my husband had stopped coming home at night. It started taking so much energy to keep up the illusion, all I wanted to do was crawl into a hole somewhere and lick my wounds. By the time I booted *perfect* Chris out, I'd gotten so good at pretending I almost had *myself* convinced everything was going to be just fine. That I didn't still love the louse so badly I couldn't breathe."

"Wait a minute. You're not actually..." Angie picked up the barking whirlwind that was the progeny of the neighbor's purebred poodle and Angie and Tony's beagle mix. She absently scratched behind its ears, the mutt's tongue lolling in canine bliss. "You don't mean you—"

"Want Chris back? Are you kidding? I don't ever want to be that perfect again."

Lissa's current plan was to be as messed up as it took to give herself and her daughters a real shot at happiness. Her mother was less than thrilled with her newfound ambition to kick butt as a single, working mother. Or with Lissa's ungracious refusal of Fanny Carter's grandmotherly offer to watch the girls while Lissa worked—that is, for the short time it should take her to find another husband to support her, so she didn't have to work at all.

But Lissa needed to do this on her own. No

husband. No parents to run home to. She needed to prove to herself as much as to anyone else that she could handle her own problems.

Laughter erupted in the den, where everyone else was inhaling ice cream, and the kids were ripping into their presents from New York. Angie's expression turned all-knowing in a way that usually meant trouble.

"You know, Tony and Martin Rhodes were out on call a few days ago," she said. "Dealing with some kind of scuffle over gang turf down by the railyard. Martin said something about asking you out to a movie sometime. I guess if you're looking for Mr. Not-So-Perfect, then—"

"Yes, Martin asked me out." Lissa and the girls had run into the devilishly charming sheriff's deputy several times over the last month. At the grocery. In the park. A bit too frequently, actually, for their friendly chats to still wash as coincidental. So when he'd finally asked her out, between the peas and the corn in the frozen food aisle, she hadn't said yes...but she hadn't said no. Martin was funny and irreverent and easy to talk to, and so many other things that serious, conservative, apple-pie Chris Fielding had never been.

"And?" Angie hadn't always liked the man, but he'd become one of her most competent officers, not to mention a close family friend who showed up at the Rivers house most weekends to play basketball with Tony.

"*And,* now that Maggie's here and I have someone besides our very nosey parents to babysit for me, I might just take him up on his offer."

It wasn't that she cared if her parents disapproved of Martin's good-ol'-boy rough edges, as much as she was sick of defending every decision she made that strayed outside the safe, refined boundaries they'd promised would make her happy.

"You and Martin Rhodes, watching a chick flick, sharing popcorn and chocolate-covered raisins…" Angie stopped petting Waggles long enough to make a show of picturing the unbelievable. "If something like that's possible after the year you've had, why is it so hard to believe that Maggie's over her guy and just down here for a relaxing summer?"

"I don't know what's up, but your niece is looking for a place to hide. And not just from a guy. Don't get me wrong. Having a nanny so I don't have to worry about the girls all summer is a Godsend. But…"

There was something a little too desperate behind the younger woman's smile and her offer to get herself out of Tony and Angie's ever-observant way. Something too eager about Maggie's wanting to spend the summer babysitting—for which she'd forever be a goddess in Lissa's eyes—instead of staying in New York and finishing the years of hard work she'd put into becoming a teacher.

"Are you telling me dating a lifetime bachelor like Martin wouldn't be your own way of hiding out?" prodded the woman who'd picked the absolute worst guy in town to fall in love with, then had proceeded to turn *never gonna work* into *happily ever after.*

"Dating Martin would be fun," Lissa admitted. "But that's as far as it'll go. I'm not looking for answers or reasons or…something to keep everyone distracted while I try like hell to pull myself together."

"And you think Maggie is?"

"With everything she's been though—" Lissa finished drying the frying pan, wondering if any of them understood a fraction of what Maggie Rivers had been dealing with for years "—would you really be that surprised?"

"LEBRETTI!" SOMEONE SHOUTED over the thud of Matt's fist striking flesh and bone. "Turn him loose, Detective."

Captain Sanders.

A second's hesitation gave the half-conscious gangster kicking and cursing beneath Matt enough time to drive his fist into the ribs Matt had bruised taking him down.

"Come on!" Matt snarled in Flores's face. "Is that all you got?"

Screw Sanders.

Screw them all.

Matt's next punch shattered Flores's jaw. The drug-peddling, gun-smuggling weasel groaned, his eyes rolling back. Then the bastard had the nerve to pass out.

"Wake up!" Matt struck again, not caring where the blows landed. "Wake up, you coward."

The piece of shit had been holed up in a rancid corner of the alley for over an hour, his semiautomatic raining a random arc of death at Matt's men. When the bullets ran out, Matt had charged from their secure perimeter.

Flores was his.

"Enough!" A set of hands grabbed Matt's swinging arm.

A brawny forearm wrapped around his neck, cutting off air and yanking him away from the gangster's battered body.

"Get the paramedics over here," Sanders

barked into his com unit. He glowered down to where two uniformed officers held Matt pinned to the filthy pavement. "And get Lebretti's ass into the back of a squad car."

"No!" Matt swallowed the vile mixture of adrenaline and rage. The blood on his face and hands slowly registered, along with the ramifications of what he'd done. "I'm fine."

Sanders shook his head, his expression disgusted—not by a punk like Flores getting beat down, but by the career one of his lead detectives had just thrown away in as public a way as possible.

"You're suspended," he said. "Get checked out by the EMTs, then get your butt back to the station. I want your badge and weapon on my desk."

The officers turned Matt loose, leaving him sprawled in the muck as they hustled to their assigned duties. The scene crawled with cops and medical personnel. Thanks to Matt's contacts and endless nights on stakeout, they'd finally brought down the local MS-13 leadership. At least until tomorrow, when a new set of soulless criminals took their place. But instead of congratulating Matt for a job well done, officers and detectives avoided eye contact, intentionally not passing too close, as if being a burnout was contagious.

Just a week ago, Sanders had all but ordered Matt to take time off. But being away from the job, the hunt, hadn't been possible. Having hours full of nothing but thinking about what he hadn't been able to do, for Bill or for Maggie, was the last thing he'd wanted.

Getting Flores had been the only thing he could focus on and not hurt. The only thing he could still do a damn thing about.

Except now that he'd brought the man down, there was no Bill to help him dig his butt out of the trouble he'd just bought himself. And there was no Maggie waiting for him at home, making him feel clean and new just because she was there.

CHAPTER FOUR

MATT HAD A COUPLE of inches of scotch left in his bottle, and no interest whatsoever in dragging himself out of his favorite chair to answer the doorbell.

But the thing clearly wasn't going to stop ringing. Whoever was out there had gotten someone to buzz him in downstairs, totally ignoring the fact that Matt hadn't bothered to.

Whoever it was better—

"Get away from the door!" he shouted, throwing back another shot of liquor, straight from the bottle.

He didn't want to see another damn person. Didn't want to think about another damn thing. Thinking only led to feeling, and feeling was at the top of his didn't-want-to-do list tonight.

He'd been off the job for two weeks. Paid leave, while Internal Affairs investigated, sounded better than being suspended. But he'd still screwed up.

And he'd let people down—his partner, his captain, Maggie…

"I'm as stubborn as my daughter, Detective Lebretti," a female with a smoky, Southern-tinged voice announced. "Don't waste our time waiting for me to give up and go away."

Only a moron would face his ex's mother drunk off his butt.

The doorbell jingled again.

Either a moron, or a man with a binge headache one jingle away from imploding.

He shoved himself to unsteady feet. After making it to the door, he worked the dead bolts, double vision creating a fuzzy mess of the locks and chains until he blinked everything back to normal. Leaning a hand against the wall, he opened up to the blond spitfire who'd raised the only woman who'd ever been able to hold her own against him.

"Mrs. Rivers, what can I do for you?"

She took in his less-than-sober state, then breezed into the apartment and rounded on him.

"To start with, you can make some coffee and drink enough of it to be able to focus on what I've come to say."

"I've got plenty to drink right here." He gave Carrinne his best scotch-bottle salute and returned to his chair. "You're welcome to join me. Glasses are in the kitchen."

She was the granddaughter of a bona fide Southern aristocrat, he'd heard—though not from Maggie. They'd never talked about their families beyond whatever was going on with them in the here and now. Luckily, in Matt's case that meant there was absolutely nothing to say, beyond the fact that his grandparents had stopped being a part of his life years before they'd both died. Of Maggie, he knew that her dad, and the uncle she left behind in Georgia, were the best cops on the face of the earth, her mother was the strongest, smartest businesswoman in Manhattan and Maggie worked her ass off hoping to make them all proud. Friends had filled in the gaps a bit, revealing that Carrinne came from money somewhere down south, even though grit and determination had won her the life she'd made since arriving in New York as a pregnant teen.

Matt could easily believe the woman's pedigree at the moment, the way Carrinne gazed down her nose at the trashed apartment he'd recently shared with her daughter. Not to mention the way he was chugging from the bottle. Then she grabbed the scotch and daintily helped herself to a good shot and a half.

Her grin as he reclaimed his booze said she knew she'd shocked him. Satisfied, she settled her petite self on top of the coffee table that matched the couch and love seat he and Maggie had picked out together.

"They look like home," Maggie had assured him in the midst of their day-long furniture shopping excursion—synonymous in most men's vocabulary for the third circle of hell. *"They look like us."*

So the bright red, slip-covered piles of padding had come home with them, and he'd pretended to like how they were too big for their tiny living area. What cop didn't want to maneuver through a blood-colored obstacle course on his way to bed at night, or when he stumbled into the kitchen for coffee in the morning? The damn things were an eyesore.

But since Maggie had left, he'd slept on them every night. Lying in their bed had been an exercise in torture. The hours dragging by, his body on fire as memories of making love transformed insomnia into erotic torment.

"Detective?" Carrinne held her hand out for the scotch. Quirked an eyebrow when he hesitated.

He shoved the bottle at her.

"When you're done, feel free to let yourself out." He waved in the direction of the door, but ended up motioning toward the bathroom instead.

Lord, he was drunk.

"Not a chance, Detective. I was dealing with my own tall, dark and brooding man when you were still trying to figure out whether or not girls have cooties. Do your worst. I'll still be here. Resistance is futile."

Hearing one of Maggie's pet sci-fi phrases come out of her mother's mouth got the better of him. His snort burned through the pounding in his head. Rubbing the heels of his hands over his eyes, he resigned himself to enduring whatever the woman had come to say. As long as it meant getting his bottle back and his ex's mother out of his apartment, so he could finish drinking himself into oblivion.

"That's right," he finally responded. "I'd heard you and Captain Rivers met when you were kids."

Maggie had shared the scrap of information only because he'd asked. Her parents certainly hadn't reminisced about bygones the few times he'd been invited to their apartment for dinner.

"Yes, we fell in love as teenagers, then we lost it all." Carrinne took another sip of the alcohol, looking like she needed it almost as much as he did. "It took my almost dying to bring us back together when my daughter was sixteen."

"Dying?"

Captain Rivers and his wife had always been friendly to him. But it's not like someone Matt's age with his background was their first choice of a live-in for their only child. Now Carrinne was itching for an overdue heart-to-heart?

"Maggie's never told you, has she?" Another swig, and she handed over the scotch, her hand shaking. "I'm not surprised."

"Told me what?"

"My daughter saved my life ten years ago. Back when she had purple hair and her eye on getting more things pierced than she's ever let me know about."

As a rule, Matt found Maggie's pierced navel was one of his favorite playthings, and he wouldn't have been opposed to her experimenting anywhere else she'd set her heart on. His body's immediate response to the images that sprang to mind left him shifting on the couch.

Get your mind off your ex's goodies and back on her M-O-T-H-E-R.

"Didn't you ever wonder where that scar on her side came from?" Carrinne demanded.

"Appendix, right?" He shrugged at her stunned

stare. "She never wanted to talk about it. Just said that she'd had the thing taken out as a kid."

"Except the scar's about five inches too long for something that simple, *Detective.* They don't have to cut you in half during a four-hour procedure that could potentially kill you in order to take out your appendix."

"She said there'd been some complica—"

"She gave me half her liver, when the doctors were giving me less than two years to live. And that wasn't the last time she put her life on the line for someone she was terrified of losing. Her best friend in Oakwood was shot and killed while Maggie sat next to her. She held Claire in her arms while the girl died, then ran with Claire's baby to protect him from the drug dealer who'd killed his mother. If it weren't for her courage and my brother-in-law, I don't know what would have happened."

Matt could only stare as shock flooded his system.

Donor surgery? A drug shooting?

What kind of bastard lived with a woman for nearly a year and didn't know—

"Sober enough yet to focus on why I'm here?" Carrinne's words dripped with disdain. "Eric and I heard from Maggie's uncle today. She's not doing any better in Oakwood than she was here.

I don't know if it's the two of you breaking up or…other things, but if there's anything you could do—"

"Maggie was pretty definite about not wanting me to do anything for her anymore." It hadn't taken her more than an hour to clear her things from the apartment.

"Or anyone else, it seems. She's spending most of her time in Georgia holed up in her great-grandfather's house, doing just about anything but seeing her family. Something's wrong. I was wondering if you knew what that might be."

"How would I know?"

Just because he'd slept with her, bought furniture with her, spent every night since she'd left dreaming about having her soft body back next to his, her laughter waking him in the morning—

"Did you know she was seeing a therapist?" Carrinne asked. "Or that bailing on her summer internship has put her on shaky ground with her professors? Her doctor left a message at our place about some missed appointments, because we're Maggie's in-case-of-emergency contact. We checked with NYU. She's behind in her course work. She dropped several classes the last two semesters."

The two semesters she'd lived with him.

"Damn." He shook his head, trying to rid himself of the alcohol haze so he could deal with the desperate mother who needed him to have meant more to her daughter than he had. He ran a hand under his chin. Two weeks of stubble bit into his palm. "What do you want from me, Mrs. Rivers?"

"Eric said…" Carrinne clasped her fingers together. "My husband said you had some downtime, and… Well, we couldn't get through to Maggie, and the rest of our family isn't having any better luck. We were wondering if you'd consider…"

Consider what?

An instant later, he was out of his chair, staggering toward the kitchen.

She couldn't be serious.

"You've spent more time with her than any of us over the last year," Carrinne reasoned. "Maybe if you saw her again—"

"I'm the last person Maggie wants anywhere near her right now."

She'd been suffering from God-knows-what, right under his nose. She was still hurting. And what had he been obsessed with? Hunting Flores and his punks, and eliminating any distractions that had gotten in his way.

"What if your trip to Oakwood was for something else entirely? What if you needed to be there on departmental business, and that gave you a chance to—"

"What business?"

"Oakwood's up to its eyeballs in gang problems the sheriff down there has never had to deal with before. He's asking for an expert to come in and consult, and Eric—"

"An expert! Didn't your husband tell you? The union psychologist thinks I have anger-management issues. Survivor's guilt. Whatever you want to call it. I'm not fit for active duty. I may be off the force for good. Since when does that make me qualified to help your daughter or anyone else with anything?"

"My husband says you're one of the best around at what you do, Detective. That his brother and the Oakwood sheriff would be grateful for any insight you could give them. I know Maggie couldn't stop talking about how amazing you were at controlling the gangs here." At his startled reaction to the compliment, Carrinne's eyes hardened. "At least until a month ago, when—"

"When she dumped me, because I wasn't there for her." When he'd been on a mission to destroy anything that had ever been important in his life. "What the hell was someone with your daughter's baggage doing with a man like me in the first place?"

He headed for the kitchen to make coffee he had no intention of drinking. Every fragile, freaked-out look Maggie had tried to hide replayed in his mind. Twisted deep inside.

"Maybe she needed to prove to herself that she could handle being with someone like you," Carrinne said as she followed. "Maybe you started out as a challenge. She's always been so determined to take on the world. Who knows? But she *did* pick you, and somewhere along the line she fell in love with you. Now suddenly it's over, and—"

"And you want me to keep on hurting her, after she wised up and cut me out of her life?"

He slammed the can of coffee to the counter. He didn't know the first thing about keeping a woman's heart, let alone mending one.

"You're the only thing my daughter's ever run from, Detective Lebretti." Carrinne trapped him in the nook of a kitchen with nothing more than the concern in her eyes. "Maybe it'll be as simple as you showing up and giving her a chance to get whatever else she needs to say off her chest. Perhaps there's more to it than that. Whether she wants to or not, I think she still needs you."

"Maggie doesn't need a thing from me." And if she did? If he tried to help, but only managed to hurt her even worse… The booze in his belly churned in a nauseous wave. "Her life started getting better the second she walked away from me."

"Really?" Carrinne crossed her arms. "Is that why my daughter had to fly over nine hundred miles to Georgia once the two of you broke up? Or why nine hundred miles doesn't seem to be far enough away for anything in her life to be *getting better?*"

"GET YOUR HANDS OFF OF HIM!" Maggie yelled from her vantage point near the back door of the Oakwood Youth Center. She sprinted to where a group of teenagers had been playing an increasingly violent game of basketball. "That's enough!"

She yanked Javier Rodriguez, the thirteen-year-old she'd been tutoring for the last two weeks, from under the older teens. Javier expressed his appreciation by spewing a string of colorful curses.

"Back off, lady!" He twisted in her grip as the older boys bolted. "I don't need your help!"

She let him go. Blood trickled from a gash where a fist had dragged his lip across his teeth.

"What you need is an ice pack, and maybe a few stitches. Most definitely a watch. You owe me a full hour of algebra every Monday and Friday, or your principal's going to bust your ass out of summer school, and you'll be repeating eighth grade in Juvie. Your parole officer calls me every week to make sure you're following the stipulations of your probation. One word from me, and you'll be doing time for that little shoplifting adventure you had at the 7-Eleven. So in addition to finishing today's lesson, you're coming back Wednesday *and* Friday now, to make sure we don't fall behind because of your basketball break."

The kid wasn't even shaving yet, but he was already almost as tall as Maggie. Give him another year, and he'd fill out into a bruiser like the boys who'd been beating on him. His kiss-my-ass stance announced he'd already figured out how to use his size to intimidate.

Maggie crossed her arms and stifled a yawn that might have been convincing, if she wasn't also covering for the way her heart was beating in her throat. What had she been thinking, agreeing to tutor at the youth center every evening after watching Lissa's girls all day?

You were thinking anything was better than more empty hours alone at Oliver's.

The quiet and the memories at the mansion, the trust work piling up that she still hadn't touched, weren't any easier to live with than nonstop family time at Tony's.

Javier and his dyslexia had seemed like an interesting challenge. She'd been happy to try and help, as a favor to a local middle school teacher friend of Angie's who'd seen something worth saving in the belligerent thirteen-year-old. Lissa's two little angels were as sweet as Southern iced tea, but reaching kids like Javier was what Maggie lived for. He was a troublemaker, but getting through to tough kids had never been a problem for her. And given her years of experience teaching in inner-city New York, the pack of hoodlums who'd attacked him shouldn't have rated a check in her back pocket for the pepper spray that doubled as her key chain.

But there she was, shaking in her tennis shoes while *Mr. Badass* stalked away, mumbling, "Bitch," under his breath.

"Wash up before we get started again," she nagged. They'd still had a half-hour's work left to do, when he'd asked for a bathroom break and disappeared outside to shoot hoops with his *friends.* "I don't want blood all over my books."

Or the worksheets she'd be sending in to update his guidance counselor.

The kid who would be spending the next twelve

months in a correctional facility without her help slammed the door after walking inside.

"Were you planning to come to my rescue?" she asked the shadows at the corner of the building.

She'd known she wasn't alone, just as she'd known Tony was there every other time he'd not-so-discreetly checked up on her.

"Is that what they teach New York City school teachers?" he asked. "That it's a good idea to confront a gang clique while they're working over a new recruit?"

Tony was still scared spitless by what he'd just seen.

He'd checked in on Maggie every chance he got since she'd started working with her new student, watching from a distance so he didn't crowd her. But a moment ago he'd been bracing to step between the two of them. Luckily, Javier had wised up and backed away from the woman.

Damn, thinking of the scrappy teenager she used to be as a woman still blew his mind.

So did the idea of Maggie tutoring one of the toughest punks in town. She had a rep for working miracles with underprivileged kids in New York. She was some kind of educational secret weapon up there, according to her parents. But some kids didn't want to be helped.

"I have a student to teach." She turned away, her skin still too pale, her gaze not meeting his.

"What are you doing, Maggie?" He grabbed her arm. "If Javier thinks getting the snot beat out of him is more important than studying with you, there's not much you can do to stop him. Next time, his pals might not give a shit about smacking a teacher down while they work him over."

"Do you think Oakwood just invented gangs?" Maggie's brittle smile was a replica of the one he'd seen on her mother years ago, when Carrinne had hit town full of secrets and the determination to handle everything herself. "I saw the tattoos on those guys. I know what the MS-13s are capable of. Just like I knew they saw you lurking in the shadows wearing your shiny Chief Deputy badge. They weren't going to touch me."

"Is that why you look ready to pee in your pants? Are you telling me they would have backed off if I hadn't been here?"

"Javier's—"

"Not your problem."

"No." She braced her hands on her hips. "*You're* my problem. I know you want me hanging out at your place more. I know my parents are worried about me volunteering at the center every night after helping out at Lissa's during the day. My mom only mentioned that a half dozen times the other night, after asking me how things were going with plans for Oliver's trust."

"How *are* they going?"

Her glare suggested where he could shove his solidarity with Carrinne.

"I'll make sure the trust money is distributed to the right organizations, however long that takes. In the meantime—" she opened her arms to encompass the building and the recreation area sprawling behind it "—this is what I do. I work with kids wherever I can reach them. If I worried about what could go wrong every time I turned around, I'd never be able to do my job."

And if she didn't sound like she was trying to convince herself she was okay, Tony would have bowed out right then and there.

Javier and his crew hadn't done any harm, not this time at least. But—

"I'm worried about you, Maggie." A whole lot of people were, and she wasn't going to like the plan her parents had set into motion to help, any more than Tony did. "You working with this kid is an amazing thing. And Lissa and her girls think you walk on water, for all the time you're giving them. I'm even okay with you doing what you have to at Oliver's, so you won't have his trust hanging over your head anymore—"

"But?"

"But, Nina tells me you're not sleeping…" Old man Wilmington's housekeeper, who along with her husband had stayed on at the mansion after his death to look after the place, had phoned him at work. She was concerned about Maggie's growing restlessness and the fact that she never went anywhere except Lissa's place or the youth center.

"From what Lissa says, neither is she. Does that mean you're having your sister-in-law tailed, too?"

"No. Lissa's life just fell apart. She's working through a difficult time. You, on the other hand, only came down here to handle family business and take a few weeks R and R, remember? Walking around looking half-dead, avoiding everyone who knows you and picking fights with Latino hard-cases doesn't sound like my idea of a summer getaway."

"I'm going inside." She headed for the building.

He held the door for her, then followed.

"You don't want to jump into the local gang scene, Maggie. If the MS-13s have already tagged

Javier, challenging them will only buy you and the kid more trouble. I've seen it too often over the last year. They'll get rougher before they let him in, just to be sure Javier can take it. That he's not too weak to do them any good. If he wants to be in the gang, he's already gone. There's nothing you or anyone else can do to stop it."

The building's air-conditioning chilled his skin as he finished. Or was it the determined look in his niece's eyes that had him gritting his teeth?

"I don't believe in lost causes," Maggie said.

She never had.

"But you hardly know this kid. And it's more than just your attachment to Javier. You've barely talked to your parents in weeks, or anyone else who cares about you. If something's wrong, why are you so determined not to let us help?"

"I don't need help!" shouted the woman who only minutes ago had calmly stood her ground against a pack of criminals. "I *need* space. And I want to be treated like the adult I've been for years, Tony. Stop babying me. I know what I'm doing."

"Really? Just like you knew what you were doing when you ditched your guy in New York to go running home to your parents? Or when you ditched them and your summer plans to come down here? Or when you ditched my family to go live in that empty mansion you're rattling around in now?"

Maggie gifted him with an enchanting view of her middle finger, then she headed for the rec room to teach the distributive property to a kid who'd hung his future on joining a violent gang, not passing remedial math.

"Don't underestimate what you're getting yourself into with Javier," Tony called after her. "My department's in over its head handling the gangs that moved in after you left. These kids are every bit as dangerous as anything you've seen in Manhattan."

"Got it." She waved absently as she turned the corner, the tattered cuffs of her boot-cut jeans swishing across the floor.

She still looked so young, she could easily be mistaken for one of the kids she worked with. But she wasn't a kid. She was a headstrong woman who clearly thought that keeping moving was the key to outrunning whatever she didn't want to deal with. He had some experience with avoiding the things he'd needed to face the most.

He'd just never for a minute expected to see Maggie following in his footsteps.

"Damn it." He yanked his keys out of his pocket and headed back outside to his cruiser.

He'd been opposed to his brother and sister-in-law's plans. Sheriff Lewis was thrilled, of course, to be getting extra help dealing with the gangs, but Tony had been reluctant to see Matt Lebretti's arrival later in the week as a good thing. The detective was a burnout only inches from losing his badge. The man had already run Maggie off once.

Lebretti coming to Oakwood was going to help how, exactly?

But Tony had seen enough of the shadows beneath his niece's eyes, and the way she panicked every time someone she loved smiled in her direction.

At this point, he was willing to try just about anything to get through to her.

CHAPTER FIVE

"DID YOU AND THE GIRLS have a good day?" Lissa dumped the groceries she'd bought onto the kitchen table, careful not to disturb the books and papers Maggie was poring over.

"Yeah." Maggie slowly looked up. She began stacking her things and smiled absently. "How about you?"

"Good enough." Putting in nine-to-five and leaving someone else to spend the day with her girls was never going to be Lissa's heaven on earth. But independence, making it on her own, felt pretty darn good. "It means a lot to know that Callie and Meagan have had you to hang out with the last couple of weeks. What's all this? Details about Oliver's money?"

"No, lesson plans—" The younger woman's cropped top didn't quite meet her low-riding jeans. The ring in her naval winked as she stood.

"For this kid I'm tutoring at the youth center. We're fitting in an extra hour this week."

"The boy Needa Cross asked you to help?" Given the pile of papers Maggie shoved into a folder, it looked as if she'd been planning lessons most of the day.

"Yeah, Javier's dyslexic, and Angie mentioned I help special needs kids in New York." Maggie hurried to the sink full of dirty dishes. "I should have gotten to these before now."

"I'll do them." Lissa shrugged out of the suit jacket that felt like it had melted to her skin, thanks to the ninety-degree heat outside. The sound of cartoons drifted in from the den. At nine and six, Callie and Meagan would live in front of the television if they were allowed to. "What are the girls watching?"

"*Cinderella.*" Maggie flashed an apologetic smile as she loaded the dishwasher. "I know I promised to take them roller skating. But I started working when their friend Bridget came over after lunch, and I lost track of time. They were out back playing for a while. When they came in for a snack, it was already after four. I gave them Popsicles and thought they could cool off with a movie."

"No big deal." There were worse things than coming home to video-induced peace and quiet.

Opening the fridge, Lissa started rummaging for useful items to throw together for dinner. Ah, she could always sell the girls on hot dogs. "Is this the same kid Tony says is getting mixed up in one of the local gangs?"

Maggie stiffened, trading dish duty for staring, as if Lissa had suddenly lost fifty IQ points. "It's for a kid that everyone else has given up on. So I'm spending a little time trying to get him to care about the future no one thinks he can have. What's so terrible about that?"

Lissa started filling a pan with water. "Nothing. I think it's great that you want to help." She glanced at the hours of work piled on the table. "As long as—"

Maggie raised an eyebrow. She looked just as capable and determined as ever, and just as lost as she had her first night back in town.

Watch it, Lissa. The woman needs a friend, not another mother.

"As long as you think you have a realistic shot at helping him. If anyone can reach this kid, I'm sure you can."

Maggie's answering smile eased the tension between them.

"Thanks. I just need to get him working instead of fighting me. He's only thirteen, but there's never been a father. He lives with an aunt, and there's no information on where the mother split to. He has to believe that he can control something in his life, anything, even if it's just algebra. Then maybe…" She checked her watch. "I'd better get a move on. I told him to meet me at six tonight."

She all but sprinted for the garage. A minute later, Lissa heard Tony's beaten-up truck rev to life and pull out of the driveway.

Angie had said Tony was worried. Maggie had started working with Javier only two weeks ago, but she'd attached hard. Too hard. And she was hyper-focused on helping him, to the exclusion of pretty much everything and everyone else.

Lissa shook her head at her friend's idea of a fun Wednesday night. If Lissa had a fancy-free evening on her hands, she was certain she could find something to get her blood pumping besides teaching an ungrateful bully. Like maybe figuring out whether or not there was anything real in all the sweet Southern lines Martin Rhodes kept throwing at her.

He'd shown up for breakfast a couple of times the last few weeks, bringing doughnuts or muffins to trade for the scrambled eggs she always offered to make. If her schedule didn't leave her time for a date, he'd teased, then he'd bring the date to her.

He never stayed long, never did anything more intimate than brushing his hand across hers, or kissing her cheek when he left.

But more was something she could suddenly see herself wanting, even though she'd probably regret it. Was *fun* with a man who'd been with just about every other woman in town really a good idea?

Still, Martin made fun look awfully tempting. Compared to the endless string of lonely nights ahead, when she had nothing more titillating to do than cleaning house and taking a good book to bed, what wouldn't seem like a grand escape?

She reached into the pantry for a box of preservative-enriched macaroni and cheese to garnish the hot dogs, but pulled up short when the doorbell rang. Checking to make sure the three adorable zombies in the den were still engrossed in their movie, she headed to the front of the house.

One second she was opening the door, the next she was gaping at the tough character standing on her welcome mat.

"Hello?"

Tall, Dark and Handsome was wearing a black muscle shirt that left his chiseled arms bare, and black jeans that molded to every muscle that bulged below his trim waist. Everything about him said danger, except those concerned blue eyes.

Dark hair… Clear blue eyes… City tough with a deadly edge…

Tony and Eric wouldn't have—

"Is Maggie here?" the stranger who must be Maggie's NYPD ex asked.

Looks like the Rivers family had indeed called in the cavalry.

Too bad their damsel in distress didn't seem the type to appreciate the finer points of being saved, whether by big, strong men, or the family going out of their minds worrying about her.

"YOU TALK TO MAGGIE YET?" Tony Rivers asked.

"She'd already left when I got to your sister-in-law's." Matt dropped his tired ass into the creaky guest chair beside the chief deputy's desk. "So I came straight here. After all, consulting with you and your men is the reason I'm down here, right?"

Rivers's cold stare blasted him.

"I'm not really sure which I need less right now—" The man stood and stepped around the desk. He didn't just look like his brother, he walked like Captain Rivers, too. "—Some burnout from up north coming into my office looking half-dead, ready to educate me about my department's problems. Or being responsible for delivering the guy to my niece, like I'm doing her some kind of favor not stopping this asinine scheme of my brother's."

Matt couldn't stomach the thought of barging back into Maggie's life, either. But he'd driven his bike sixteen hours straight, stopping only for fuel, thinking of nothing but the woman he hadn't helped when he'd had the chance.

"Asinine or not, I'm here," he said. "I can spend all my time trying to do whatever I can for Maggie. Or while I'm in the area, I can help with your gang situation." Not that he was certain he had much to offer. "Either way is fine with me, so make up your mind."

"Well, when you put it that way—" Tony's smile promised retribution if Matt stepped one foot out of line with either the man's niece or his backwater sheriff's department. "How can I pass on such a generous offer?"

YOU HARDLY KNOW this kid....

The kid that had shown up for tutoring that evening, long enough to tell Maggie where she could shove her painstakingly prepared lessons. Then he'd left with the same gang of hoodlums who'd pounded on him Monday.

So, there she sat in her great-grandfather's

study, hours later, surrounded by the mountain of applications Oliver's lawyers had received from foundations and individuals wanting a piece of the Wilmington Trust. Proposals waiting to be carefully read and considered, all of which she'd avoided for weeks, so she could focus on her grand plans for Javier Rodriguez.

Curled up in Oliver's enormous leather chair, her black leggings and Happy Bunny T-shirt screaming that she didn't belong amidst priceless antiques and shelves filled with first-edition classics, she threw down the real estate offer a broker had faxed over. Oliver's law firm had advised that the best thing to do was sell the mansion, then reinvest the capital in the trust. Now a generous offer had dropped into her lap, all wrapped up with a bow and ready for her to sign.

Except, she couldn't.

She kicked her legs to the floor and disentangled herself from the chair. She hadn't just avoided the trust applicants so she could help Javier, or before that so she could finish her degree. She hadn't felt qualified to decide what her great-grandfather's legacy would mean. And she hadn't wanted to say goodbye—to a man who'd been gone for over a year.

What had Oliver been thinking, putting her in

charge of all this? What had she been thinking, coming down here, deciding to stay in an echoing old house with just the man's housekeeper and her husband for company?

She'd been so sure that what she needed was quiet and some time alone to get herself back on track. Suddenly, quiet and alone sounded like a coward's way out, all prettied up so she didn't have to face the truth.

The only thing she'd achieved by avoiding her Oakwood family for two weeks was ensuring that no one but Nina saw her becoming completely useless.

Brave. Strong. That's what her friends and family thought she was. What she'd been so sure she was. She could handle anything. Deal with anything.

Except, she couldn't.

Executing the trust was supposed to be something she was honored to do. In the midst of everything else she was failing at, she could have felt good about Oliver's memory and investments living on through the foundations and charities she chose to help. But just like the therapy she'd only stuck with for a few months, handling Oliver's legacy made her skin crawl. The impulse to be anywhere else was even stronger. She wanted to run again…but run where?

She jumped at the sound of the doorbell. Heading toward the front door, she heard Nina's footsteps in the hallway.

"I've got it."

She swung the door open, gasped, then just as quickly slammed it shut. She growled as Nina, who was swathed from the neck down in the daisy-covered chenille robe she wore over her nightgown, joined her. Then she left the housekeeper to play hostess and took the stairs to the second floor two at a time.

Grabbing her cell phone off the vanity in her bedroom, it was a wonder she didn't break the thing as she ripped it open and speed-dialed the current bane of her Oakwood existence.

"This is Rivers," her uncle's semialert voice slurred after he picked up.

"Are you dimwitted or just stubborn?" She checked her watch and winced at the time. A baby began wailing somewhere in the background. A woman's voice cursed. Several dogs joined in the commotion, barking happily.

Maggie refused to care.

"What part of back off and let me live my life don't you understand?"

CHAPTER SIX

MATT HAD REACHED the bottom of the steps fronting the mansion's palatial porch by the time the door opened again.

"Don't tell me you came all this way just to give up without even seeing her," an elderly voice challenged.

He turned beside one of the six columns bracing the second-floor balcony and frowned at the woman who could have been any age from her early fifties to eighty. Gray sprinkled her ebony hair. Lines told their own story around her eyes and mouth. But the determined way she held the door open made it clear she was more than capable of coming after him, if he chose not to heed her gracious welcome.

"You must be the detective from New York." She didn't seem particularly surprised to find him on her porch at close to midnight.

"Did Tony Rivers mention I'd be coming?" He retraced his steps, reaching out his hand.

"Something like that." She shook, then waved him inside. "It's still close to eighty degrees out there. Don't let out all the store-bought air."

Absurdly anxious to do as he was told, just as confident it was a bad idea, he stepped into the artificial coolness of the house.

"She's upstairs, if you're planning on going after her." The older woman fussed with the ties to her robe.

He shook his head and rubbed his hand across the back of his neck. He was grimy all over and in desperate need of a few hours' sleep.

So why have you been driving around the block for hours?

"My name's Nina."

"Matt Lebretti."

"Oh, I know all about you, Detective. All I need to know, at least."

"Then you'll understand why following Maggie upstairs isn't the best idea."

But stalking her all the way down here from New York makes perfect sense!

"Come on, then." Nina sighed and headed down a spacious hallway. "You look like you could use some strong coffee. We'll wait and see if the princess makes an appearance."

Princess?

Oddly enough, that's exactly what he'd thought the first time he'd met Maggie. She'd been a city girl wearing nothing fancier than shorts and a tank top, her hair dyed jet-black instead of the smooth chocolate it was now. But still, she'd been magnificent. Too young, too beautiful, so clearly someone's princess. So out of his league. And he'd been chasing her ever since.

"What can I get you?" Nina asked as he followed her into a kitchen large enough to prepare food for half the town.

"Nothing, really. I should be go—"

"Detective..." She raised a spatula in a way that suggested she wasn't afraid to use it.

"Um, coffee would be great."

A crash from the front of the house, followed by a victory whoop, had him running back down the hall.

"Good Lord," Nina cried, hurrying after him. "What was that?"

He sidestepped the brick that had been thrown through the stained glass set in the top half of the front door. Noticing there was something wrapped around the red projectile, he only spared it a glance as he pulled the door open. Vaulting off the porch, not bothering with the steps, he raced down the sloping lawn, reaching the curb in time to see taillights, as a truck squealed through the Stop sign at the end of the square. The back fender was conveniently license-plate-free.

When he turned back toward the house, an angry woman was waiting for him at the door, and she wasn't wielding a spatula. A woman who'd taken everything decent in his life when she'd walked away.

Maggie had grown thinner over the last few weeks. Older, perhaps. And her eyes. The haunted eyes he'd remembered, the ones he'd glimpsed only briefly when he'd gotten there, still had the power to break his heart.

She glanced down at the brick she held in a shaking hand, then back up as he approached. Checking out the note taped to it, he shoved his hands into his pockets to prevent them from pulling her into a hug she'd hate him for.

Butt out, Bitch! the note's jagged handwriting demanded.

"Friends of yours?" He walked around her and back into the opulent mansion he'd been hesitant to enter before.

She could follow or not. She could avoid him all night, if she thought it would get her anywhere. But he wasn't leaving. Not until he knew exactly what kind of trouble she'd gotten herself into down here, and what the hell her uncle was doing to stop it.

"YOU DID WHAT?" Matt demanded.

He continued pacing in front of the kitchen table where Maggie sat, those crystalline eyes softening as his voice hardened.

Why had she let herself be dragged into this conversation? And why was Nina still there, insisting that they both could use something to eat?

"I'm tutoring this kid at the youth center," she repeated, fingering the brick she'd set on the table. It beat looking into eyes that got to her each and every time. "Helping him, and Monday—"

"You helped him out of a gang beating?" Even angry, rumpled and in need of a shave, Matt looked good enough to eat, no matter what part of his body her gaze landed on.

Speaking of eating, how long did it take to scramble a few eggs and butter the wheat toast Matt preferred over white?

"Shouldn't you be getting to bed?" Maggie asked the ever-helpful, ever-present housekeeper who'd recently morphed into an odd cross between a fairy godmother and a nanny. "Carl's been asleep for hours."

And Carl slept like the dead. There was no chance of him waking up and helping Maggie talk Nina into giving her and Matt some privacy.

"The detective looks like he hasn't eaten all day, and I'm guessing you haven't, either." Nina turned back to the stove. "This won't take long."

"I'm sure Matt can find something to eat wherever he's staying." Maggie had been trying for cool confident as she not-so-subtly suggested that Matt show himself to the door.

The quiver of *please* in her voice ruined the effect.

"Actually." He crossed his arms, his pacing coming to an abrupt end. Only two insignificant feet separated them now. "I doubt they're still up, even if dinner did come with the bed they offered me as part of the agreement to consult with the local sheriff. I wouldn't want to wake anyone over there this time of night."

"They?" The sensation of being smothered was rising again. As unwanted as the instant spurt of joy that had flooded her when she'd opened the door to find Matt standing there. As destructive as the panic that had quickly followed. "Consulting? Please tell me, my family… My uncle—"

"Your uncle and his boss are out of their element dealing with the gangs down here. Your father knows my captain well enough to ask for a favor. And…" Matt's confident stance drooped in a very *un*tough guy way. Folding his arms, sighing, he slid into the chair beside hers. "And I was looking for a couple of weeks away from the task force, anyway."

"Wh-what? Why?" He never missed work, for anything. "N-never mind."

His decisions were none of her business anymore.

"I didn't want you to hear I was back from someone else," he said.

Bullshit.

She squinted, letting her eyes shout the expletive, because a disapproving sigh from Nina about her language was the last thing she needed.

"Have you forgotten my cell number already?" Accusation bubbled up, as she realized how far her family had gone. How messed up she must really seem, for them to have tried to pull something like this. Her body was shaking again, but no longer because someone had been pissed enough to throw a brick at her house. "More to the point, Tony could have told me you were coming one of the dozen or so other times he's just happened to run into me this week!"

"It wasn't definite that I was coming until yesterday." Matt crossed and uncrossed his arms, a pretty good sign that she wasn't going to like what he said next. "Let's just say your mother wasn't taking no for an answer."

"My mother?" she squeaked. Lord, she sounded like Minnie Mouse. At least the way Minnie would sound, if she were fantasizing about killing her sneaky, rodent parents. "My mom thought it would be a good idea for you to follow me down here to—what did you once call Georgia—*Southern-fried hell?* You can't be serious."

"I think I'll head on to bed." Nina presented Matt a plate piled with not just eggs, but sausage and warmed-over biscuits from that night's dinner. A feast the domestic diva had slapped together in ten minutes flat. "The real estate agent's bringing over a representative from that Savannah girls' school in the morning. They've been making noise for months about buying this place for their West Georgia campus. I'll have to be up early, making sure everything looks its best."

Breezing away from the tension in the room as if she was leaving them to chat about the weather, she patted Maggie's shoulder on her way by. Her arched eyebrows could have been a commentary on anything from Matt's drop-dead gorgeous face and body, to Maggie's less-than-ladylike fury.

"I didn't call," Matt said when they were finally

alone, "because I didn't think you'd talk to me. And I decided to come by tonight because I had no intention of chasing you all over town to the amusement of your entire family. I...I had to see you, Maggie."

"Well you've seen me, and I'm fine. You should be all set to work on whatever you need to with my uncle."

His grim stare wasn't an encouraging sign.

"Matt—"

"I don't know what you think you're playing with down here," he cautioned. "But just because you're not in Manhattan, doesn't make things like gang violence any less dangerous."

Dangerous?

Dangerous was wanting to lean closer to him and beg him to hold her until the sound of shattering glass stopped echoing through her mind. Until images that had nothing to do with the here and now evaporated.

Gunfire.

Claire crumpling to the floor. Her baby screaming.

Blood everywhere.

God, get a grip!

"I...I'm fine," she repeated. "It was just a teenage prank."

And what happened to Claire had happened a lifetime ago.

"It was a warning from a gang that's as violent here as they are anywhere else. The MS-13s nearly kill new members when they initiate them. You getting in their way because you're distracted by all the other crap you're dealing with has given them a shiny new target. You're not going to be *fine* until we've neutralized whoever's got you in their sights. And I don't care how badly it pisses you off, I'm not going anywhere until I'm sure that happens."

The edge to his voice was shocking enough. But the anger vibrating there, when he was always so determined to stay under control, reminded her of how he'd talked about hunting down Bill's killer and making sure the guy didn't have a chance to hurt anyone else.

Still, it wasn't his unwanted overreaction to a stupid brick that had her gaping like an idiot.

All the other crap you're dealing with...

The safe place that part of her still fantasized he could be—the safe place he'd once been without realizing it, *because* he didn't know every last thing about her the way her family did—was gone forever.

Someone, no doubt her mother, had taken even that from her.

"Get out and don't come back." She stood. Headed for the stairs, her cutting glare daring him to follow. To keep looking at her with the softest expression she'd ever seen on his face. "And when you talk with my parents again, when you see my meddling uncle, give them a little message from messed-up, too-weak-to-know-what's-good-for-her me. They can all go straight to hell!"

CHAPTER SEVEN

MAGGIE'S TIRES SQUEALED the next morning as she braked at the curb in front of Lissa's house. The sight of the squad car in the driveway had her blood boiling.

What, now Tony was ambushing her? But the serial number on the cruiser finally registered. It wasn't her uncle's unit. Most likely, Martin Rhodes had stopped by for more coffee and another eyeful of Lissa's generous smile, among other things.

Damn it! Giving Tony the bitch-slapping he deserved would have been a fine way to start the morning. He'd refused to talk to her when she'd woken him last night, saying only that she should think about what Matt had to say.

Oh, she'd been thinking all right. She'd had the entire night to think.

About Matt and Tony and Javier. About a lot of stuff. And what she thought was that she'd had enough. She could let a stupid brick scare her away from doing her job. She could hole up in the mansion for however long Matt was in town. She could put off dealing with Oliver's trust forever. But somewhere around four that morning she'd decided that she'd done enough hiding in New York to last a lifetime.

She'd come back to Oakwood to get on with her life. It was time she learned whether she really had it in her to help kids like Javier. Not to mention if she could finally let go of the past—which now included her great-grandfather's house as well as Matt Lebretti. Especially Matt Lebretti.

Grumbling under her breath, she shoved herself out of the truck and headed for the house, letting herself in through the garage without knocking. The door wasn't locked. Doors in Oakwood seldom were. Though what she saw, the shock and obvious embarrassment on the faces of the two people springing away from a passionate clench beside the refrigerator, was a pretty good argument for protecting your small-town privacy.

"Oh!" Normally unflappable Lissa blushed from her dainty ears downward.

"Yeah, um…I should be going." Martin Rhodes contemplated the toes of his department-issued loafers, both hands thrust in his pockets. "Er, thanks for the coffee."

He nodded to Maggie as he passed, in a kind of John Wayne way that had worked for the Duke, but not so much for Martin. Maybe if the Oakwood deputy had a hat he could tip or something…

"Sorry about that," Lissa said once he was out the door.

"No worries." Maggie threw the backpack that passed for her purse onto the counter by the sink, rattling the cookie jar it settled against. "It's your house. You can do what you want."

Lissa, in the process of wiping off the traces of smeared lipstick, stilled at Maggie's tone. "Are you okay? I tried to call last night, but—"

"I wasn't up for chatting."

The woman who'd been a neutral friend, amidst the craziness of the last few weeks, sighed as she sat at the table and smoothed the wrinkles from her skirt. "He came here first, you know."

"Who?"

"Your detective from New York. He showed up right after you left for the youth center. I'm sorry, maybe I should have called you, but—"

"You're sorry? You knew what my parents were up to, and—"

"I didn't know anything until he rang my doorbell, Maggie." Lissa actually sounded hurt. "I told him you weren't here, sent him on his way, then by the time I got the girls fed and into bed no one was answering the phone at the Wilmington place. I figured he'd already found you, and—"

"Mom, why are you still here?" Callie stumbled into the kitchen, her red-gold hair curling madly in her sleepy eyes.

Good timing, considering what she would have walked in on a few minutes earlier. Lissa and Martin had clearly expected the girls to stick to their sleeping-late summer schedule.

"I'm heading out for work now." Lissa gave her oldest a peck on the cheek and, with motherly indulgence, nudged her toward the den and the thirty minutes of cartoons the girls were allowed to watch before breakfast.

There was no motherly indulgence in the look she gave Maggie.

"I don't have a clue what your family's up to. I know they're worried about you. Honestly, so am I. But I wouldn't go behind your back. I respect you too much for that. When I've got something to say, I'll say it to your face, trust me."

Maggie absorbed Lissa's assurances, blinked back the anger that had risen so quickly, and so unfairly. She'd just attacked the one person in town who wasn't treating her like a scared little girl.

"I'm sorry." She sat beside her friend. "It's just that…"

"It's just that it sucks to have everyone around you wanting you to be okay and watching every move you make, like they don't trust you can solve your own problems? I know."

And she did know. Lissa had been living in her family's version of a fishbowl for over a year.

"I think my parents are done watching," Maggie mumbled. They thought she'd gone completely 'round the bend. "But why send Matt down here? How on earth is that going to help?"

"I thought you were over him." Lissa picked at the tablecloth.

"Yeah, me too."

"Maybe—"

"There's no maybe." Not for her and Matt. "I can't… Us being together…it doesn't work. And no one knows that better than Matt."

What was he doing, stopping by the mansion to see her, saying he was worried about her, after the way she'd dumped him?

"Then you have nothing to worry about. Martin said Matt would be briefing the deputies on gang intervention all week. Stay out of his way, and he'll stay out of yours."

"Yeah." Except Matt hadn't looked like he had space on his mind when she'd stormed out of the kitchen last night.

"Hey, you okay?" Lissa gave her hand a squeeze.

"I'm fine. I have a lovely day ahead with Callie and Meagan, and more planning to do for my tutoring, even though my one and only student flipped me off last night. What more could a girl ask for?"

DRIVING THE FEW MILES to the bank, Lissa kept waffling between worry over Maggie and the humiliation of being caught groping Martin Rhodes. As if she were a child who needed to hide anything she was doing.

Except she didn't feel so much like a girl who'd been discovered in an inappropriate clinch, as she did a woman who'd just had a taste of something she wanted to do again…soon…really, really soon.

One minute, Martin had been sucking down his second cup of her freshly ground French roast and suggesting that they take the girls on a picnic this Saturday—*so* not a thing anyone in Oakwood had ever seen Martin waste a free weekend doing. He'd smiled in embarrassment when she'd said as much.

"I guess I'd do just about anything to get you to spend the afternoon with me," he'd responded, taking visual inventory of her from head to toe in a way that announced that he'd be open to much more than the park, if she was ever willing.

And evidently, she was.

She'd reached for him in that blind, starstruck way of lovers in romance novels. Those happily-ever-after stories she'd stopped reading right about the time cheating, lying Chris had stopped paying any attention to her. At her touch, Martin's teasing grin had melted, and like heroes of old, he'd pulled her against him and taken control of the kiss, their friendly morning coffee and her girls waking up just down the hall completely forgotten.

Thank God, Maggie had barged in before Callie or Meagan had gotten a peek of Mommy losing it over someone besides the daddy they both still loved to death.

She screeched to a stop at a red light, a horn blaring from the car behind her. The toys, books and other kid debris littering her backseat slid to the floor.

She couldn't remember the last time she'd

kissed her ex-husband with that much abandon. Or wanted anything as much as she wanted another taste of Martin. The man was no doubt looking for a fun, meaningless fling, while she had fairy-tale love stories on the brain.

What had happened to the harmless diversion she'd described to Angie? A man had actually responded to her as a woman, and she'd completely lost her head after just one kiss.

Sighing, she pressed the accelerator the second the light turned green. She couldn't keep Maggie's last words out of her mind. Her young friend had even more people worried about her than Lissa did. And after seeing Matt Lebretti again for the first time in weeks, she'd been doing as bad a job of *no big deal* as Lissa was after kissing Martin.

"I'm fine," Maggie had said.

Weren't they all!

"DEFINITELY a gang skirmish," Lebretti said as he surveyed the rail yard Friday morning, dressed in the same black-on-black street attire as when he'd driven into town.

"How do you figure?" Sheriff Lewis followed until they were beside one of the torched railcars.

A few steps behind, Tony was absorbing everything their supposedly burned-out gang consultant said and did.

The guy had slept nearly twenty-four hours straight, amidst the nonstop noise and mayhem of Tony's home. And from the looks of the dark circles under his eyes, Lebretti was still several weeks short of being at his rested best. Fatigue hadn't stopped him from getting on with the job, though. He seemed steady enough. Sharp, in fact. The more the detective talked about Oakwood's gang situation, the more engaged he became.

"The graffiti's from two different factions," Matt continued. "The rail yard's probably a prime location between your town and the next one over, this Pineview you told me about. These markings here—" He pointed to a circle spray-painted on the side of an abandoned storage unit, filled with symbols that had been nothing more than gibberish to Tony and his boss "—They seem pretty typical of the ones we see in New York, when one gang calls another out. The MS-13s you have were staking a claim. Looks like another group had different ideas."

"Claiming what?" Lewis wiped sweat from his eye. "Drugs? That's what this all seems to be about. Who sells them, who brings them in. Random violence has been escalating for years, along with the drug convictions, but nothing like what we've seen in the last six months."

"Most likely Oakwood's clique of MS-13s had themselves a nice little small-town operation. Gangs don't always involve themselves with the drugs directly. They're probably handling the dealers that were already here. Taking a tax in return for protection. Making sure runners and shipments get where they're going. Securing themselves a nice fifty percent off the top while staying one step away from the illegal activity. But say the area popped up on someone else's radar, or MS started expanding into the county over toward Pineview. You said it's an African-American gang in control over there—probably some set of either Crips or Bloods. And say some big-city leader decided to move money and power down here and see what he could do about the MS-13s thinking they've got the neighborhood locked up. That's all it takes."

"So they're fighting over money?" Tony didn't like the proportions of the kind of *skirmish* Lebretti was describing. "You make it sound like business."

"Big business. Money, control, territory, it all means the same thing in a gangster's world—*respect*. Without control over an entire area and the respect of the dealers that are running up and down your state, national gang networks can't stay in business. They survive through intimidation and by destroying anything and anyone who gets in their way. By taking whatever money they can and making sure whoever keeps the rest knows who's protecting their interests."

"You sound pretty confident there's more than one gang in play." Lewis was MBA-educated. A smart, no-nonsense man always focused on the facts. Lebretti had his undivided attention, and if Tony was reading the conversation right, the captain's on-the-spot respect.

Their on-loan detective scanned the destruction that had stalled Oakwood rail shipments for several days until the tracks could be cleared. Tony could sense him absorbing the details and formulating an opinion based on his years of experience.

Like hell the man didn't care whether he walked away from gang intervention, either here *or* back in New York.

"They'll bust up everything in their path until one gang dominates the other," Lebretti said. "Two gangs representing interests in the same territory is a recipe for more of what you already have. The violence will get worse and less out-of-sight the longer the tension escalates. Stockpiling money and weapons is common. Extreme demonstrations of loyalty will be demanded, from both members and the riffraff they protect. Basically, your department's control over the situation will continue to splinter, as long as this county and the next are in play. And any innocent bystanders that get in their way are going to get hurt."

"Innocents like Maggie?" Tony asked.

Lebretti hadn't said much after leaving Maggie Wednesday night, except that he didn't think there was any way to trace who'd thrown the brick and its message at the mansion.

"Maggie?" Lewis turned to Tony. "Your niece?"

Tony and Matt's gazes locked. Officially bringing Maggie onto the sheriff's radar could mean all kinds of complications. But what choice did they have?

"There was an incident at the youth center Monday," Tony explained, "with a kid she's tutoring. A group of Latino boys, most likely MS-13s, were roughing up Maggie's student. She stepped in and stopped it. Then someone threw a brick through one of the Wilmington mansion windows Wednesday night."

"And you think the two are related?"

"Yes, sir," Matt answered before Tony could.

"But as long as she does the smart thing and steers clear of this Rodriguez kid, she should be okay."

Lewis inclined his head toward Tony. He'd hit town only a little over a year ago, but by now he'd heard the stories of Maggie's teenage exploits.

"Is your niece going to do the smart thing?" he asked.

Tony sighed at the combination of anger and concern clouding Lebretti's expression. He was a man who supposedly didn't care about anything anymore, neither the job nor Maggie.

"No, I don't think she'll do the smart thing," Tony admitted. "Not where protecting a kid like Javier is concerned."

Lewis nodded silently as he scanned the destruction around them. He was a by-the-book officer that Tony respected without reservation. But there'd never be anything by-the-book about the way Tony would protect his family from the kind of danger Maggie had exposed herself to.

"Well, then I suppose you should be finding out everything you can about this kid she's teaching," the sheriff said. Registering the shock Tony couldn't quite hide, Lewis shrugged. "If he's linked to the MS-13s, maybe the information will get your niece to see reason. And Lord knows, we need every scrap of intelligence we can get to figure out what the hell to do next."

MATT DIDN'T LIKE THIS. Maggie was going to freak. Again.

But her showing up to tutor Javier again after what had happened earlier that week made no sense. And after what he'd seen at the rail yard, and the new information Tony had just uncovered on the kid, the stakes were too high for Matt to stay out of it. If she was headed for another run-in with the MS-13s, then Matt's place was standing between Maggie and anyone threatening her.

"You don't trust me with her, do you?" he asked the brooding cop leaning against the cruiser beside him. Both of them were sweating like a son-of-a-bitch in the late-afternoon heat, while they waited in the youth center parking lot. "Have you stopped to think that you could save yourself a lot of hassle by letting me be the bad guy here? Why give Maggie two targets to be pissed at when she comes out of that building?"

Tony's sideways glance said no, he didn't completely trust Matt with his niece, but he was growing more amused with the situation by the minute. "You be the bad guy all you like, Detective. Think of me as moral support. Once she's done venting her spleen at you, Uncle Tony'll be there to agree with every nasty thing she has to say about you. And hopefully to talk some sense into her once she calms down."

"You people thrive on ass-backward down here, you know that?" Except Tony's small-town good cop, bad cop might just work.

"We're like bulldogs taking care of our own, if that's what you mean." Tony chuckled, then his expression hardened. "But if you don't have the guts to do what needs to be done, then take the squad car and head back to the station. Lewis is over meeting with Dillon Reed, Pineview's sheriff. I figure you've got about an hour before he's back and wanting to talk your ear off some more."

If the gangs are all that's important to you, Tony's stare added.

"I'm not going anywhere," Matt countered. "But take my word for it. Forcing Maggie to talk about something when she's not ready just makes her run."

And the thought of being the cause of more of the panic she fought whenever he was nearby had kept him away since Wednesday night. He'd figured she was safe enough locked up in that monstrous house.

Now here he was, ready to blast the distance Maggie needed straight to hell.

Another squad car turned the corner and pulled into the youth center lot, coming to a halt beside Tony's.

"Martin," Tony said when the imposing officer stepped from the second cruiser and removed his mirrored sunglasses. "This is Detective Lebretti."

The large man took Matt's hand in a beefy paw.

Large wasn't the right word. This wasn't an overmuscled, steroid-enhanced pretty boy. Rhodes was built like a NFL linebacker, but his size was in total proportion. Matt got the impression of speed and athleticism. Of strength and intelligence and an unconscious, natural ability to intimidate everyone around him.

In short, the lieutenant was the kind of cop you wanted standing next to you while you informed the town's newest gang member that the teacher he and his buddies were threatening was off-limits.

"So, the MS-13s finally tapped Javier?" the bruiser asked Tony in a way that rang with years of familiarity.

"This morning, evidently." Tony jerked his head toward the beaten up truck Maggie drove. "Don't know if he's in there with her, but Maggie's been meeting with him every Monday and Friday evening. I'm guessing we've got another twenty minutes or so before she finishes up."

"You think Javier's the one who broke the window over at the Wilmington place?"

"It fits," Matt replied, "now that we know they're initiating him. They'd want proof of loyalty, and he's close enough to Maggie to make an example of her. If Maggie's a mark, Javier won't stop with just a brick. If he doesn't want to become a victim himself, he'll have to follow through as publicly as possible."

And no way was Matt letting that happen. He wasn't delusional. Whatever chance he had with Maggie was gone. But she was going to be safe. He owed her at least that much.

"Lissa said Maggie's pretty hung up on this kid," Martin said.

"Did she?" Tony grinned at his deputy. "What did you do, drop by last night and offer to take her and the girls out for pizza?"

"No." Martin didn't grin back. "We had coffee this morning."

"Yeah," Tony said, nodding. "Lissa makes a mean cup of coffee. It's a wonder half the department's not offering to help her finish her pot every morning, now that Chris is out of the picture."

If the angelic-looking woman Matt had met the other day was unattached, it wasn't hard to imagine the local boys lining up at her door.

"You planning on having someone escort Maggie home every Monday and Friday night, until she wises up and cuts this kid loose?" Rhodes rested back against the car, his stance casual enough. But his jaw was clenched.

"Something more important pressing for your time?" Tony asked.

The deputy settled deeper against the cruiser. He crossed his legs at the ankles and ignored his chief's dig.

So there they stood, as mismatched a bunch of modern-day musketeers as Matt had ever seen, waiting to rescue a woman who most definitely wouldn't appreciate her role as their damsel in distress.

They were one for all, and all about to get their heads handed to them by the angry beauty emerging through the building's front door.

CHAPTER EIGHT

"WHAT DO YOU MEAN, *good?*" Maggie demanded as she gawked at the trio of more brawn than brains standing in the parking lot. "What's good about Javier not being here? He's throwing away an entire year of school, and with it his chance to stay clear of the system. All because he'd rather hang with a bunch of gangster wanna-bes who're going to keep beating on him until he's *cool* enough to be one of them?"

She'd spent the last two days talking herself into facing Javier again, meticulously going over her lesson plans, only to arrive and find the kid a not-surprising no-show.

"It's good, because those other boys are the real deal, not wanna-bes." Tony moved away from his squad car. His big brother, big bad deputy, *whatever!* mask was firmly in place. "And according to a source of mine, he's already involved with them enough to be a threat to you."

"And the three of you are here to do what, exactly?" She barely let her gaze flicker to Matt before it locked onto Martin, then swiveled back to Tony. "Protect defenseless me from a thirteen-year-old?"

"We half expected Javier to turn up tonight with a few of his buddies along for the fun," Martin replied.

So far, Matt had been smart enough to keep his mouth shut. She was suddenly spoiling for a fight, and he was too convenient a target standing there in his city clothes, reminding her of every amazing thing she'd once had in New York.

"What?" she fired at him now. "Did you think they'd challenge me to a game of basketball, and I'd just innocently follow them out back like a stupid little lamb? I've taught in schools patrolled by cops and armed guards! I heard what you and Tony said the other day. I can take care of myself."

"And what if Javier had shown, and he'd been on his best behavior, then he'd offered to walk you out to the truck?" Matt's expression tightened. "Maybe he'd tell you he needed to talk, and he didn't have anywhere else to turn. Would you have said no then? Would you have been ready for the *friends* he'd have had waiting out here with more than a brick this time?"

Maggie swallowed as the picture he painted formed in her mind. She squeezed her eyes shut against images of another messed-up teenager she hadn't been able to help.

Blinking, she forced her shoulders straighter, refocusing on the kid she might still have a chance to save, if she could just get through to him.

"I don't believe Javier would intentionally hurt me."

"To score him an in with the MS-13s, he'd do just about anything." Shadows deepened Matt's blue eyes. "I've seen people killed for less. Cops killed for less."

The way Bill had been killed… Bill and Claire and maybe Matt one day… Tony… Her father.

"Listen to the man," Tony urged through what sounded like a long tunnel. His words echoed off the fear closing in on her, smothering her, refusing to go away no matter how deeply she breathed or willed it to stop. "I can't say I care for what I've heard about Matt's problems with the NYPD, but he's been dead-on with everything he's told us about these gangs. What happened Wednesday night at the mansion might only be the start. Until we know for sure where Javier stands, it's not safe. Steer clear of—"

"Safe!" God she hated that word.

She laughed, and Matt tensed at the sharp sound.

She'd once turned to him to feel safe.

Then she'd run from him for the same reason.

Just like she was running now, not realizing she was doing it until she heard Tony's curse behind her.

"DAMN IT." Tony started after Maggie, but Matt grabbed his arm.

"Let me go," he said. "You said you wanted me to be the heavy."

He walked off, not waiting to see if Tony followed. It was all he could do not to start sprinting himself. But seeing him barreling after her wasn't going to do Maggie any good.

Besides, he needed a minute or two to figure out what the hell he was going to say next, since he'd handled everything else so perfectly.

I say I love you because that's how I feel....

Well, she hated him now. The look in her eye as she'd told him off Wednesday night, then again just now, couldn't have made that clearer. He knew everything her family knew, and then some, which made him the enemy. And he'd give anything to just let her go, the same way he had in New York.

Except she was in danger now. And she was deliberately exposing herself to more, trying not to lose this kid to the MS-13s.

She could run all she wanted. She could keep insisting that she could handle things on her own. But neither Matt nor her family were buying it anymore. The only person still willing to believe that she was okay was Maggie herself.

He found her near the basketball courts, her back to the building, sitting on the ground with her head buried in her hands. He'd never seen anyone look so…lost. A word he'd never thought he'd use to describe this amazing woman, or himself.

But he was lost, too.

If she ran, he'd be fast on her heels. Tony's sheriff could demand another briefing that very second, but Matt would be right where he was, chasing after Maggie. Looking out for her until she was strong enough to see that she wasn't taking care of herself.

He'd never known this kind of urgency. Nothing in his life had ever mattered as much as making sure Maggie Rivers was okay. Not even the job he'd been so certain he couldn't live without.

"Why are you here?" she asked before he'd worked up the nerve to say anything.

"Why are *you* here?" He squatted beside her.

The paleness of her skin drew him closer, but he knew better than to touch. “Why come here to tutor this kid, when you know it’s not safe? Sounds like chances were good he wouldn’t even show to begin with.”

“Because…because I can help him,” she said in that hiccuping kind of way of someone whose control was shredding. “And I don’t give up on the people I can help.”

“What about when you need help?” Something she’d never accepted before now, according to her family. “You needed it in New York, didn’t you? And coming down here hasn’t changed anything.”

She lifted her head, betrayal filling dry eyes she hadn’t let fill with a single tear.

“My mother has a big mouth.” Maggie stood with the easy grace he’d always admired.

She didn’t push herself up with her hands or struggle against the wall. She didn’t reach for him and the support he’d have been happy to give. She just braced her feet on the floor and stood, the muscles in her deceptively trim figure working to get her where she needed to be.

And for the first time, that drive to stand on her own left him furious.

“Your mother’s worried about you,” he bit out, standing as she wrapped her arms around her body, her hands brushing at chill bumps that defied the late afternoon heat. "Your whole family is."

"Well, I don't want them to be, so they're off the hook." Maggie tried to push past him.

He grabbed her arm.

"*I'm* worried about you."

"Since when?" She yanked away. "Since when are you worried about anything, except strangers on the street who're easier to care about than the people in your life?"

His gut tightened. He deserved every word and more.

"Maybe since I'm off the force, and I've had some time to think."

"What do you mean, off the—"

"Suspended, pending an IAD investigation."

Something close to understanding transformed her frown into concern, and the urge to kiss her nearly broke free. To hold her in his empty arms and make something feel right for the first time in over a month. But she wasn't his to hold or kiss anymore. He'd made sure of it.

"Did you get him?" Her eyes softened along with her voice.

"Yeah, I got him. I found the bastard who ordered the hit on my team, and I damn near killed the man with my bare hands. If I'm lucky, the DA won't come after me. But I'm not sure there's much chance of saving my career. I don't even know if I care."

"I..." She did the unthinkable, and reached for his hand. Squeezed his fingers. "I'm sorry."

And she was.

No matter that he'd ignored her problems and shut her out, Maggie's bottomless heart was still capable of being genuinely sorry for *his* loss and pain.

He pulled her to him gently, refusing to remember that he shouldn't. And when she slid her arms around his neck instead of breaking free, the compassion and comfort of her hug stole the last of his control.

His fingers cupped the back of her head, her sun-warmed hair sliding across his skin, the sensation causing his hands to clench into gentle fists. She stiffened, and he groaned. She was finally coming to her senses and pulling away.

But instead, she raised her head from his shoulder and arched her neck into his touch. Opened those mesmerizing eyes and gasped at the hell that must have been written all over his face.

I've missed you, his brain refused to let him

say. *I never knew how much I needed you until you were gone.*

The words would have given him comfort, maybe a chance to win her back, but he refused to be that selfish. To fight to be something to her again, when she'd be better off without him.

"Matt?" she asked. Her lips parted on his name, their softness only inches away.

Torturing him, she inched even closer and sealed her mouth against his.

Her kiss wasn't the sweet, delicate offering of a Southern flower. It was the all-consuming demand of the New York woman who'd laid siege to his life and left her generous, passionate mark behind once she left. Her hands roamed over his sweat-dampened shirt, then clenched around the muscles of his upper arms as he found the curve of her butt with his own hands and lifted her against him.

The softest part of her nestled against hardness that demanded he turn and press her against the brick wall behind them.

"Baby, don't," he somehow managed to say as his palm cupped an unconfined breast covered only by the colorful tank tops she wore layered one on top of the other. "Not if you don't want me right here, right now. It's been too long. I need you too damn much."

I need it all!

The silent demand seared through him. He crushed his mouth back to hers, taking away her ability to tell him to stop. Not that he had to worry. Her kiss, her body's reaction, was as free as the wind, and full of the same desire driving him.

Her hand trailed downward between their bodies. He grabbed her palm and pulled her to his straining flesh.

She wasn't ending this. She wasn't turning away. Despite weeks of silence, and the chasm of misunderstanding still between them, she wasn't any more over him than he was her. The realization consumed him as completely as her taste.

A discreet cough and the approaching crunch of shoes against gravel made them both stiffen only a second before—

"Maggie?" Tony rounded the corner of the building and came to a sudden stop.

Matt gentled his hold on the quivering woman he'd been a minute away from nailing against a rough, brick wall. He eased her to her feet and guided her behind the shelter of his back. While she fought for balance, he locked eyes with her uncle.

"Everything all right?" Tony's Southern drawl didn't detract from the sharpness of his expression.

But the man looked more interested than angry.

Matt had no idea how to answer. Saving him, Maggie stepped forward, her hand lingering on his arm, branding his skin.

"I'm fine," she said as she let go. She lifted her chin, renewed determination sparkling in her eyes. "And I don't want to hear another word about me not helping Javier. From either of you."

Her unsteady gaze met Matt's.

"Maggie…" He wasn't buying how quickly she seemed to have pulled herself together.

Too much still simmered just beneath all that calm. He wouldn't have taken the time to see it in New York. Now he couldn't see anything else.

"You'd be taking too big a risk," Tony warned. "Assuming the kid ever shows up here again. It's not an option. I—"

"Not an option? Risk?" She moved farther away. "What do you call what you do every day, Tony? You know the dangers, but you keep doing your job. You have a family, and you know what could happen when…when…?"

Tony stepped forward, only to stop when Maggie backed up even further.

"It's not the same, honey," Tony reasoned. "Matt and I are trained to deal with the kind of violence we face on the job."

"And I'm trained to deal with at-risk teenagers." The mutinous tilt to her chin dared either man to deny it. "If you're ready to give up on Javier, you go ahead. I'm not. Not until I talk to him myself."

"He'll probably be armed." Matt fought back the memory of his partner's blood-covered face. The feel of Bill struggling to breathe in Matt's arms, then suddenly no longer moving at all. He wasn't letting that happen to Maggie. "Meeting with you might be just what his handlers want him to do. You're an easy target, coming in and out of this place."

"Like you and Tony and his deputies aren't targets, parading all over town, meddling in the gang's business?" Her sarcasm couldn't hide the tears filling her eyes. "Like any of you couldn't be gone in a second if someone wanted you out of the way. God! It doesn't even have to be a gang. Or a gun. It could be…it could be anything, and…"

She slapped a hand over her mouth as if she were about to throw up. Swallowing a sob, she turned and ran again, this time toward the rusted truck she'd left out front.

Tony Rivers looked ready to tear something apart as he rounded on Matt.

"Do you mind telling me what the hell's going on with my niece?" he demanded.

"Damned if I know." Matt headed after her, feeling the weight of what he did know settling more heavily on his shoulders with each step. "Except that dealing with whatever's terrifying her gets harder every time I'm around."

"I SHOULD BE OVER THERE." Tony was pacing with newborn Sarah in the nursery while Angie tried to rock Garret to sleep after a bad nightmare.

They spent more time in the kid's room these days than they did their own.

"Maggie doesn't need one more man telling her what she should be feeling tonight." Angie kissed Garret's head, the tenderness of the gesture only one of the million reasons why Tony would love this woman for the rest of his life. "Nina said she was fine when I called."

"You didn't see how upset she was at the center. And it's not just over Matt being here. Or the three of us showing up to warn her about Javier."

"Yeah, that plan was a stroke of genius." Angie's soft snort unsettled the nearly sleeping child nestled on her chest. She smoothed their son's curls. "You, Lebretti and Martin ganging up on a grown woman, thinking she'd be grateful for your total lack of confidence in her judgment about the type of kid she's been trained to help."

"I'm not sure even Maggie trusts her own judgment right now." Sarah's cries had softened to snuffling whimpers that would have lulled a less-experienced parent into putting the baby back in her crib. Not fooled, Tony continued to rock and pace. If he put the little angel down now, there'd be hell to pay. "One minute she's practically spitting in Lebretti's face, the next she's all over him."

"She's a big girl." Angie understood his special bond with Maggie better than most. His wife had been there when Maggie had finally learned to trust him, and when he'd realized how much more she meant to him than merely being his brother's long-lost daughter. "If she's making a mistake with Matt, she's got to figure that out for herself."

"And what if *he* isn't the problem?"

Matt hadn't revealed anything when Tony pressed for details. He'd spent more time with Lewis that evening, discussing what to expect as tensions between the local gangs escalated. But details of what was going on between the detective and Maggie had been off-limits.

That kind of loyalty had the guy growing on Tony.

"Maggie's fighting off the people who care about her faster than we can figure out how to help," he reasoned out loud.

His wife gazed at him through the room's shadows, her frown full of memories. Time was, they'd been the ones running from anyone who got too close, especially each other.

"I know," he agreed in response to her silence. "I can't fix this for her. But I don't care how responsible she feels for this kid she's been tutoring. The trouble Rodriguez is courting isn't getting anywhere near Maggie again. I'd be over at the Wilmington place now, if Lebretti hadn't already planned to watch the mansion every night this weekend."

"That'll last about as long as it takes for Maggie to figure out he's lurking around."

"He's not going anywhere." Tony had seen enough to trust the detective's commitment to protecting Maggie. He gently laid a sleeping Sarah in her crib. "If Maggie somehow manages to run him off, I'll have another cop stationed under her bedroom window from dusk 'til dawn until we're certain Javier's no longer a threat."

"I'd like to be a fly of the wall when you explain that one to Lewis. The same way you're going to have tell him Matt's using one of the extra squad cars all weekend, so anyone who approaches the house will know it's under surveillance." Angie rose from the glider rocker and slid

Garret into the twin bed across the room from the crib. "You know I was always a pushover when one of the guys used departmental resources for personal business."

"Are you saying you're not worried about Maggie, too?"

"Of course I'm worried about her." Angie floated toward him, her floor-length, cotton nightgown glowing in the moonlight and drawing his hands to its softness as she relaxed into his arms. "But you can't force Maggie to feel better, or work things out with the man she loves, or to follow whatever rules you think will keep her safe."

"I could lock her in jail until she comes to her senses."

A tiny part of him was serious. But when Angie's lips began kissing a path across his bare chest, he suddenly couldn't think beyond how her breasts were pressing against him like cotton-covered clouds.

"Hmmm...another good career move, Chief." She wound her hands around his neck and tugged his head closer, until her next words whispered across his lips. "Why not let Detective Lebretti take the watch for a while?"

Tony kissed his wife, the urge to hold her close as strong now as it had been the first time they'd touched over seven years ago. The same kind of never-let-go desperation he'd seen in Matt Lebretti's eyes as he'd tracked every move Maggie made that evening.

It was hard to accept that a stranger might be his family's best chance at reaching Maggie, but it was looking more and more like Carrinne had been right on point with Lebretti. Tony just hoped to God his niece started trusting her NYPD watchdog, or someone else, soon.

CHAPTER NINE

MAGGIE NEEDED… She needed…

She needed everyone to back the hell away!

Right. 'Cause spending your entire Saturday alone is working wonders on your disposition.

She walked down an aisle of the mansion's solarium, trying to drink in the peaceful sounds of summer chirping away just beyond the glass windows. Whatever the rows of seedlings and bedding plants around her required was provided here. This room was a nurturing oasis that had fascinated first her mother as a child, and then Maggie when she'd fallen in love with the place as a teenager.

The promise of planting something helpless then watching it thrive under her care had been an awakening for a city girl who'd always scoffed at her mother's love for green things.

Maggie had spent as much time here as she could during the two years she'd lived in Oakwood, especially those last few months before she'd left for college. After Claire was gone and Angie was healing from injuries she'd gotten while helping Tony protect Maggie and Claire's baby. After the final shoot-out had sparked a daily struggle not to give in to the nightmare of everything Maggie had seen and done. Everything she hadn't been able to stop from happening.

When the pressure to be okay had made it impossible to breathe anywhere else, she'd always been able to come here. Somehow, being in this place her mother had always loved had helped her heal. Given her the strength to move on to the future she'd wanted so badly. At least that was the lie she'd told herself.

In truth, this place was where she'd first learned how to run. She'd isolated herself in the warm shelter of this room instead of facing what had happened.

And this morning, when hiding in her great-grandfather's office, ignoring last night's meltdown at the youth center, ignoring everyone's worry and Nina's attempts to get her to eat, hadn't resulted in a single productive decision about the Wilmington Trust, the solarium was where she'd escaped to again.

Turned out running was the only thing she seemed to be good at anymore. Even when she was running from Oliver's final wishes, and the town that was supposed to be her last safe place to land.

Tears blurred the solarium's illusion of peace. She fumbled in her jeans pocket for her cell phone. Scrolling through the menu of contacts, she selected the estate lawyer's private number and pressed Send.

"Bradley Granger," the deep baritone at the other end of the connection answered.

"Mr. Granger, this is Maggie Rivers." She shoved her bangs out of her eyes and headed back into the air-conditioned coolness of the house. "I hate to bother you on a Saturday, but I'm finally trying to make a dent in all this paperwork. Do you think you could spare a few hours to bring me up to speed on the different funds and charities who've applied for designations from the trust?"

She couldn't help but grin at the man's relieved, "Absolutely!"

"Nina?" She poked her head into the kitchen after she ended the call. "Mr. Granger will be over in about thirty minutes. Could you bring some sandwiches and coffee to the study? I'm afraid I'll be holding him hostage for several hours."

"I think I can pull something together." The older woman took inventory of Maggie's scruffy, sleep-deprived appearance. The smile that spread across her face made it clear she saw something beautiful, regardless.

"I'm heading up for a shower," Maggie said as she turned away.

It was time to fish or cut bait, and stop clinging to her final ties to the crotchety great-grandfather who'd won her heart. Time to make his final requests a reality.

She'd promised to babysit Lissa's girls that evening. It looked like Martin Rhodes had earned himself a night on the town. By the time Lissa arrived with the kids, Maggie intended to have made legitimate progress in her plans for this place and Oliver's neglected assets. The rest…

She wasn't anywhere near ready to go there today, not after the panic and memories that had attacked at the youth center. A meltdown triggered in part by the arrival of a man she'd never been able to safely hide her heart from. Not her heart, and not the mixed-up emotions that filled it.

But she had to start somewhere, before she woke up one day and realized that she'd run from her entire life.

"SO, YOU'RE FINALLY giving Martin a little somethin' outside of your kitchen?" Maggie asked after

Nina had ushered Callie and Meagan away for fresh-baked cookies.

Lissa shot her friend a look that wasn't quite a smile.

It had been a spur-of-the-moment decision, asking Maggie to sit tonight. Then it had taken most of the afternoon to work up the courage to call Martin and ask him to a movie. Lissa had almost talked herself out of it more than once, especially after she'd heard what Maggie had been through at the youth center yesterday evening.

"Are you sure you're up to this?" she asked, and not just because she was still looking for an excuse to call tonight's plans a really bad idea.

"Why?" Maggie's loaded question vibrated with frustration. "Are you worried I can't handle the girls all of a sudden?"

"No." Lissa channeled her oldest's *are you nuts?* stare. She walked to the mirror mounted over the marble hall table and went to work smoothing the wisps of hair set free by the day's humidity. "It's my impression that you could handle just about anything you set your mind to. Which begs the question..."

She bit her lip.

Leave it alone, Lissa.

"What?" Maggie had been on edge since they'd

arrived. Now she looked as if she was spoiling for a fight. "If you're talking about what happened at the youth center yesterday—"

"Yeah, I heard about that." Lissa abandoned the hopeless exercise of arranging her curls into something resembling the sophisticated style other women mastered so effortlessly. "Angie was fuming when she heard what Tony and Martin pulled with your detective. I wasn't really surprised. Your uncle can be a little myopic when it comes to deciding what's best for someone he cares about. But what I don't understand is why you didn't tell those three mountains of testosterone to go to hell."

Maggie started to respond, then stopped. A deep sigh sucked the life out of her agitation, leaving behind a woman Lissa would hardly have recognized if she hadn't witnessed the transformation first hand.

"I…I tried." Maggie's admission sounded almost juvenile. "I just couldn't… It's not just Javier, or Tony and Matt not thinking I can handle him… I—" She sat in the gilded chair beside the table. "I keep seeing things, Lissa. Flashes from a long time ago. And having that happen while I'm trying to deal with my family…with Matt…"

"You mean what happened to your friend when

you were a teenager?" Lissa's heart almost stopped at the guilt and pain washing over Maggie's features. "That was forever ago."

"Yeah." Maggie wiped a hand over her face, regaining a bit of her usual composure. "Eight years and two weeks."

"Honey, why haven't you talked to anyone about this?"

"What makes you think I haven't!"

"But not your family, I'm assuming, since they're spinning their wheels trying to figure out what's going on."

"No, I can't—"

"Or this guy who drove nine hundred miles or so to make sure you're okay."

"God, no."

"But you're talking to me about it?" Lissa didn't know whether to be honored or scared, if Maggie thought she had the answers after totally screwing up her own life.

"You're… It's…" Maggie stood. "It's different. I don't have to worry about letting you down."

"You mean to tell me you think there's anything you could do to disappoint your family, after all the amazing things you've done, after everything you've survived?"

"What if I'm not a survivor?" Maggie's question echoed down the mansion's two-story hallway. "What if I'm not handling any of this? I've been back here for weeks, and today's the first day I've even been able to look at Oliver's trust. He's been dead for over a year, and I still can't let him go."

Lissa bit the corner of her mouth to control the urge to wrap her arms around her friend and indulge in some good ol'-fashioned mothering. Maggie already had a mother, one she didn't think she could turn to at the moment. Lissa knew a little more about that than she cared to admit.

"I always thought you were smarter than this," she said.

"What?" Her friend's suspicious gaze seemed to be trolling for any hint of judgment.

"I know what it feels like to have people think you're perfect, and refuse to see you any other way, because they can't handle the reality that you have flaws. Your family doesn't expect you to be perfect, Maggie. They're harassing you to talk about what's bothering you. All the difference in the world."

Maggie sat back down.

"I… I've never wanted them to see… I've always been able to—"

"Fake it?" Lissa nodded. "Yeah, I dug my own

grave with that one, too. It only made it worse when I finally tore off the mask and owned up to all the *me* underneath. I just had farther to fall in the end, because I'd been too much of a wimp to own up to who I really was."

"You mean your parents don't approve of the divorce?"

"The divorce, they're embarrassed about. Me not already being halfway down the aisle with Mr. Perfect Number Two has been their biggest disappointment ever."

"That's just stupid." Maggie was incensed.

Lissa might just have to hug her after all.

"As stupid as thinking a family as great as yours can't accept a little weakness to go along with all that kick-ass you've got in you?"

Maggie seemed to be trying to swallow her next words before they could escape. "What… what if it's not just a little? What if…"

Lissa took her friend's hand and squeezed.

"The people who love you are either going to accept the bad stuff, along with all the good, or they're not. Pretending to be what you think they want, when the truth is tearing at you like this, is only going to get harder, until eventually you won't be able to keep up the lie. It just might surprise you who'll end up seeing you the most clearly."

Maggie's sly smile was a refreshing change of pace.

"You mean like Martin sees you?" she asked.

"Maybe." Lissa ran her hands down post-baby hips that were only smooth thanks to panties made by the angels of Victoria's Secret.

She hadn't decided exactly how closely she wanted to be seen yet.

"Well, take your time tonight." It was good to hear Maggie laugh. "I have Disney as my secret weapon if board games fail. Lots of clothes up in the attic to try on, too. You know, if you and Martin wanted to—"

"We're not going to do anything but a movie tonight. Maybe a late dinner. That's enough excitement for this single mom."

Now who was hiding?

So she didn't practice what she preached. Getting serious, then having Martin's interests cool the same as her ex-husband's had, sounded like a good enough thing to hide from. What Maggie didn't know wouldn't hurt her.

Just like Maggie didn't need to know that the one person on earth who seemed most determined to accept her exactly the way she was, was parked down the street in an Oakwood cruiser.

MATT'S FINGERS WRAPPED around his Beretta, his palm automatically finding its place on the grip, a split second before a badge flashed outside his window.

"You should probably leave your cell number with the station," a familiar voice drawled.

Tony Rivers walked around the front of the squad car, then knocked on the passenger window. Matt flipped the locks, and the door opened. Rivers bent to find him holding his gun in a now-relaxed grip.

"Things'll go a mite smoother for you in small Southern towns," Tony advised, "if you don't take down the chief deputy who's bringing you hot coffee and subs. Mind if my friend joins us?"

"What?" Matt stowed his gun in its cubby between the seats as the back door opened, too, and Rivers and Deputy Rhodes joined him in the cruiser. "Has something happened with the MS-13s?"

"Nothing much." Tony rummaged in a paper sack while Rhodes opened a thermos of rich-smelling coffee. "Nothing the department can't handle on its own until tomorrow. So we figured we'd come spare you a spell."

Rivers produced a paper-wrapped sandwich. A cup of coffee was passed forward from the backseat, which Tony took when Matt still hadn't moved.

"Look—" Matt began to say.

"No, you look." Tony thrust the cup and sandwich at him until Matt didn't have a choice but to take them. "As much as I agree that someone should be keeping an eye on this place at night until we know more, you've got to be nuts to think you can do it indefinitely by yourself."

"I caught some sleep yesterday and today." Matt threw the sandwich onto the dash but couldn't stop himself from drinking down half the coffee in a single, scalding gulp. "God, that's good."

"Two nights in a row?" Tony pulled out more subs and handed one to his deputy. "A couple hours shut-eye in between? I'm figuring your brain'll be mush by the time Lewis wants you back in his office in the morning."

The smell of spicy cold cuts filled the car as the other men began to eat. Matt's mouth watered, but he'd be damned if he'd dive into Rivers's food, as if he hadn't had the sense to pack something before he headed back over that afternoon.

Which he hadn't. He'd been too tired to do more than move from Point A to Point B.

"I'll be fine," he said.

"You're right," Rhodes said through a mouthful of food. "He is as stubborn as a southerner. There may be hope for him yet."

"Yeah, unless he's too much of a hardcase to take help when it's shoved under his nose." Tony grabbed the discarded sandwich and did just that. "Eat. Get some sleep. We'll keep an eye on things for a few hours."

Matt jerked the food out of his face, bestowing an eat-shit glower on its provider.

"You may be in love with her," Tony reasoned as he turned to watch the front of the Wilmington mansion. "But she's my niece. You might as well eat, 'cause it'll be hours before you get rid of us."

Silence ticked the minutes away, except for the sound of two grown men enthusiastically enjoying their food for Matt's benefit. Giving in before he started drooling, he ripped the paper off one end of the sub and took a healthy bite. He managed not to groan as the mixture of flavors burst to life in his mouth.

"I care about what happens to Maggie," he said after inhaling another mouthful. "I'll do whatever it takes to protect her. But I never said I was in love with her."

And there he had his problem, clean and simple. If he couldn't find it in him to love someone like Maggie Rivers, he really was as dead inside as he'd always assumed. And she deserved better.

A snort of laughter came from the backseat. Maggie's uncle shook his head in the passenger seat.

"I know you were pissed by what you saw us doing Friday." Matt's body responded to the mere memory of having Maggie back in his arms. He studied Rivers's nonreaction before continuing. "I just want you to know, I didn't come down here to pressure her into anything."

The other man nodded as he crumpled his empty sandwich wrapper.

"The thing about my niece," he said, "is that she's a grown woman, as my wife has reminded me frequently this weekend. I don't need to know anything about Maggie's personal life, except that she's safe and happy. Neither of which is the case at the moment, whether you pressure her into anything or not."

Matt chewed the last bite of his own sandwich, letting everything Rivers had said, and everything he hadn't, sink in.

"Pushing's not always so bad," Rhodes said from the back.

Tony chuckled. "Is that so? I heard you didn't get much further with Lissa last night than some movie-time necking."

A sandwich wrapper sailed forward to whack Rivers upside the head.

"Sometimes you gotta figure out what you want and make your intentions known, is all I'm saying," Martin explained. "The ball's in Lissa's court now, and maybe she'll take a pass. But at least I know I stepped up to the plate."

Matt felt his mind drifting as the banter continued around him. Sharing stakeout duty was always better than putting in the time alone.

It had surprised him more than once since arriving in Oakwood, the way he found himself remembering why he'd joined the force in the first place. To make a difference, which he already had down here, by bringing the locals up to speed on the information and insight he'd forgotten the rest of the world didn't know by rote. And to serve with others who shared his passion for protecting communities—like the two men arguing away in a car that had been oppressively silent before their arrival.

The need to sleep had been pressing hard for the last few hours. Finally, he let it take him, trusting the other officers without question. As different as the three of them were, where it counted, they were exactly the same.

As he dozed, memories of Maggie returned. Her taste. The sensation of running his hands over every inch of that amazing body.

He'd promised to let her go. What they'd become scared her too much when he couldn't guarantee her he'd be around tomorrow.

There'd be no more kisses.

No more pressure.

But at least I know I stepped up to the plate....

Martin Rhodes's philosophy of love was Matt's last waking thought before the blackness took him.

MAGGIE WALKED AROUND the side of the house, leaving the back gardens behind, not stopping until she'd reached an enormous cypress tree.

She'd sifted through the bulk of the trust proposals, it was after three in the morning, but still she couldn't sleep. Lissa's advice from last night kept nagging at her.

If she'd just trust people to see her the way she really was, she might be surprised who ended up seeing her the most clearly.

Except there'd be no surprise. She'd already walked out on the one person with a direct line to her heart. And what had he done? He'd followed her down here and made her want him all over again.

She sat beneath the ancient tree that had been her mother's favorite as a child. The limbs above her rustled, as if an old friend were kicking back and saying hello. She smiled in spite of everything.

"Maggie?"

She shrieked, jumping to her feet before the owner of the deep voice registered.

"Matt? What the hell are you doing lurking around here?"

Hadn't he had enough?

"I've been watching the house." He stepped closer, his eyes narrowing when she instinctively moved away. "It was late, so I decided to check out the grounds while I cleared my head."

"Watching the..." She was going to kill her uncle. "You know, just in case my childish display on Friday confused you, I'm not so messed up I can't sleep through the night without someone keeping an eye on me."

Her trembling, little-girl voice was back.

"Go away, Matt." She turned and headed back to the house.

"Not a chance."

If she hadn't heard pity, she might have kept on walking. Instead, she threw herself at him, catching him totally off guard and shoving him backward.

"Stay away from me!" She pushed again, only

this time he was ready for her. Shocked, but ready. He didn't budge as he grabbed her hands and forced them to her sides. "Let me go, or I swear I'll scream."

She could feel it building. A sound she didn't want to hear any more than he did. She'd given up thinking she could hold it in forever, but she'd be damned if she was coming unglued in front of Matt again.

He loosened his grip, his chest heaving.

She hugged herself.

"You tell my uncle I don't need your protection or his." What she needed, she couldn't get from anyone else—a speck of the confidence and courage she'd inherited from her parents, but had lost so completely over the last eight years. "If I want to help Javier, I will. If I think he's a danger to me, I'll remove myself from the situation. You and Tony have far more important things to worry about than me."

Matt opened his mouth to say something, then closed it. He dropped his head and stared at the toes of his favorite motorcycle boots, weighing his next words in a way that was totally out of character. As out of character, she thought, as having him watch over her all night, instead of scouting out the gang situation he knew so well.

"I'm part of this." He gestured between them. "Whatever this is. Whatever you've been dealing with since before we met, I'm part of it now. I'm not backing off until I'm satisfied that you're safe, and I don't give a damn whether you agree to having help or not. You're too off balance at the moment to listen to reason. The sheriff has a gang battling with one the next county over. And the kid you're trying to help is in the middle of it. We don't know which way this is going to go down, but someone's likely to get hurt before the local authorities regain control, and that someone's not going to be you."

"I'm safe here." As safe as she felt anywhere. "I haven't left the house all weekend."

"Someone tossed a brick through your window and threatened you, you're so safe."

"And Javier didn't show for tutoring Friday. Once I report that to his parole officer, he'll be picked up. He'll no longer be a threat to me or anyone else. The kid has no reason to come anywhere near me again. So no worries. Life is good. One more teenager is lost to the gang violence no one seems to be able to control, but at least I'm *safe!*"

IF MATT UNDERSTOOD anything now, it was that Maggie Rivers hadn't felt safe in a long time. Too long. He stared up into the midnight sky. The array of stars winking back at him seemed surreal compared to the emptiness that lay beyond Manhattan's skyline.

He'd woken from a three-hour nap feeling better than he had in weeks. Satisfied that he wasn't going to nod off again, Tony and Martin had left him the Thermos of coffee and headed home to grab a few winks of their own. And when Matt had stumbled across Maggie sitting so forlornly beneath that damn tree, he'd taken a total stranger's advice and decided to push.

"You mom said you were eighteen when you lost your friend, Claire." He closed a hand over Maggie's arm, offering the understanding and support that he'd convinced himself he hadn't needed after Bill's death. And look where that had gotten him. "I know this Rodriguez kid is even younger. But you did everything you could eight years ago, and you've done everything you can now. Stop feeling responsible for something you have no control over."

She swallowed convulsively. Her bottom lip trembled, reminding him that understanding and support weren't all he wanted to give her. Not now. Not a million years from now.

But he wanted Maggie to be okay more.

"Baby, you have family here. And parents back in the city who are desperate to help you. Do you know how lucky you are? Tell them what—"

"Lucky?" The night sounds around them stilled at her shout, before resuming the humming, hypnotic cadence he'd barely noticed until it was no longer there. "I'm *lucky* that the people who've always admired me finally get to see how screwed up I am?"

"You're not screwed up!" Where the hell had she gotten an idea like that? *Where do you think, Lebretti?* "You're hurting, and you have every right to be after what you've been through. Anyone who tells you different is just plain wrong. *I* was wrong. It's no wonder you're upset, with all the crap you've had to deal with. And you needed someone to listen. I should have been there for you in New York. But I was too messed up with my own stuff over Bill."

He threaded his fingers through the hair tousled around her face. When her lips trembled against his palm, and her eyes flooded with the moisture he'd never get used to seeing there, it was more than he could stand.

He'd never kissed a woman so gently, hoping his touch would somehow mend what he'd helped break. He'd never had a woman cling to him the way Maggie's hands were grasping his shoulders now. He didn't know how to give her the tenderness she craved, but he was damn well going to give it his best shot. Even when he knew she'd likely turn away from him again.

Her soft, almost apologetic moan as she wrapped her arms round his neck broke his heart. She'd needed him, his body and his acceptance, and he'd pushed her away.

He didn't have the strength now to do anything but pull her closer. They'd been reckless back at the youth center, starving to satisfy the desire to touch and taste, after depriving themselves for so long. But this…this was savoring. Crawling to a cool brook and drinking, coming alive once more, and never wanting to leave the oasis they'd found.

He cradled her, his hands soft on her back, when nothing about him had ever been soft before, not even for her. Their tentative kisses were all the more devastating because of the fire trembling though both their bodies, demanding something faster and deeper. But there was no place for a rough drive for completion, when the moment they were creating was so perfect it couldn't end.

God, what would he do when it ended?

"No," she whispered brokenly into his mouth.

"Shh." He soothed, his hands rubbing up and

down her arms. He had no idea what he was doing, but he was desperate to make something better for her. He kissed a path along her jaw. Her head nestled against his shoulder as if that's where it belonged. "It's okay. I'm here. I'm not going anywhere."

"No!" She was out of his arms so fast, he stumbled forward. "Don't you say that to me, damn it!"

"Maggie…" He had to have her back in his arms. He needed—

"Go away." She was shaking her head, not really looking at him. "I…I need you to go away."

"I'm not leaving you like this." The way he'd left her alone and hurting too many times. "I know I let you down—"

"No!" Haunted brown eyes locked with his. "Don't you get it? It's not about you. It's not your partner's death, or my job or my family. It's not Javier or anything in Oakwood. It's me. Me! All you wanted was a woman who could handle simple, everyday things like letting you do the job you've been doing for years. All anyone else has ever expected me to do is get on with my life. And I…I can't. I can't handle any of it. I've been pretending for so long, I let myself think everything was fine. But I…I can't make it stop…I…"

"Can't make what stop?" he asked even though

he'd pretty much figured out the answer over the last few days.

How many cops' families had been through the hell of getting on with life after suddenly losing everything in their world that made sense? Since 9/11, how many of them had pretended they were okay? Only they'd lost the ability to carry on with everyday things like going to work and keeping up friendships, participating in the communities that no longer brought them peace, or venturing into the city that could never be home for them again?

He'd been trained to recognize delayed stress in his men. To refer officers to departmental intervention to help them and their families with a condition that was so commonplace on the force, no one thought twice about it anymore. Why had it never occurred to him that someone as put-together and brave as Maggie Rivers could be having the same kind of shattering reaction that had stopped some of the toughest men he knew in their tracks?

He'd thought she was afraid of his job.

The woman was afraid of her life.

"I can't stop any of it!" she flung back at him. "I can't make any of it go away. I keep seeing…I keep hearing…until I can't eat or sleep, or…or be with you, or with anyone here, I just…I can't!"

The shock on her face told him he was the first person other than perhaps her doctor that she'd admitted any of this to. That maybe she hadn't even faced it fully herself before tonight.

"I couldn't do any of it," she continued, so lost in her thoughts that she hadn't yet realized he was holding her hand again. "I couldn't concentrate on schoolwork. Being with my students wasn't working. I couldn't be with you or my family in New York, or at Tony and Angie's, and now I can't stand being here, either. It's…it's too hard to be…to be—"

"Normal?" he asked.

It seemed to be both the right and the wrong thing to say. She tried backing away. He held tight.

"Stop it," he begged. She tugged harder. "Stop pulling away. It's okay—"

"Okay!" She stilled in his grasp. A strangled laugh escaped her disbelieving smile.

"It will be, baby." It had to be. She couldn't live like this. "But you have to let someone help you. If you can't do that here, then we'll—"

"No. I'm done running." The sober statement had the hair rising on the back of his neck. "I'm finishing this. Dealing with my great-grandfather's trust, working with Javier, even if all I can do is report him to his parole officer and let the system take over. Maybe that's the best way to keep him out of this gang, I don't know. But I have to see this through. Your dedication to your job was one of the first things I fell in love with, Matt. Don't ask me to be satisfied with abandoning my own responsibilities. I've already done enough of that."

Her eyes sparkled in the moonlight. She'd never looked more magnificent. And he'd never wanted more to be able to promise her all the love she deserved.

"Maggie, I—"

"I'm going back inside. And I'll set the alarm behind me." Her bravado faltered as she wiped at her eyes. "Thank you for…for listening, and for worrying about me. But don't. You're right. I *am* going to be okay, whatever it takes."

He watched her jog toward the house. When she was out of sight and there was nothing left but the darkness surrounding him, he dug his hands into his pockets and stared at the manicured lawn beneath his boots. Not finding the answers he sought there, he tried looking up into the sky again, only to find his view obstructed. The delicate branches and foliage of the tree he'd found Maggie beneath spread out above him like a canopy. A few steps allowed him to lean backward against its trunk.

He didn't really believe the woman who'd just run from him was okay, any more than he believed she'd completely given up on Javier Rodriguez. So he was going to keep an eye on this place while she was alone here at night, then he and Rivers would keep track of her during the day. Maggie deserved to be protected. She always had, whether she wanted it or not.

And she deserved to be loved.

He'd been with her for over a year, held her in his arms night after night. But he'd never given her what she really needed.

And now he might never get a second chance.

CHAPTER TEN

WHEN LISSA got home from work on Monday, Maggie was on the phone.

"You haven't seen him since Friday?" Maggie was asking. She winced at whatever answer she received. "Any idea where he might be? I'd like to speak with him again about tutoring. He's throwing away his chance to advance with his peers next year, not to mention violating the conditions of his probation."

Lissa had been relieved that morning when her friend seemed her usual self. Maggie had said she'd spent the weekend making decisions about the Wilmington Trust. She'd smiled as Lissa admitted that she and Martin had mostly ignored their action movie Saturday night and engaged instead in some satisfying theater groping. Everything had seemed fine as Lissa headed off to another day at the bank.

Now, it sounded like they were back to square one.

"I understand," Maggie said into the phone as

she turned her back to Lissa. “You have my number. Please call me if you hear from him? I don’t know how long I can hold off his PO, but I’ll do my best. Javier was making real progress. He’s got a good shot at catching up with the kids in his class, if he’ll just stick it out and do the work. He’s a bright boy and—”

Her shoulders slumped as the person at the other end evidently hung up.

“If this Javier kid wants to self-destruct,” Lissa said, wiping at the puddle of crumbs left over from the girls’ afternoon snack, “you might just have to get used to the idea of letting him.”

Maggie finally faced her, resignation and guilt dragging down the corners of her mouth. Her slow blink and *not you, too* expression didn’t exactly bode well for the rest of what Lissa was about to say.

She’d done a lot of thinking since Saturday, about her friend’s determination to handle everything by herself. And her increasingly alarming mood swings, which so far Lissa hadn’t mentioned to anyone. One minute the woman was sweet as punch with the girls, the next she looked ready to tear something up or burst into tears.

It had to stop.

Lissa had been so sure that Maggie was starting to see that.

"Sometimes things are just going to end messy," she said now. "And that's okay. A little mess isn't so bad. Everyone'll learn to deal with the mess. So will you. Unless you drive yourself crazy fighting something you can't change."

"If I could just talk to him one more time, or maybe—"

"It doesn't sound like that's going to happen. Who was that on the phone, the parents?"

"No, Javier lives with his aunt. She hasn't seen him since Friday."

"Then that's that. Call Needa Cross. Let her contact the parole officer if you don't want to."

"No, there has to be another way to deal with this. I don't just give up on kids because it stops being easy to reach them!"

"How about when it starts being dangerous?" Lissa sputtered.

If she didn't watch it, she was going to have to find herself a new nanny, *and* a new friend.

"It was just a brick!" Maggie stood and began riffling through her backpack. "And nothing else has happened since then."

"Probably because you've had an NYPD detective camped outside your house every night, parked at the curb in a sheriff's department cruiser."

Maggie looked up, a piece of paper clutched in her hand. "I'm well aware of where Matt's been all weekend. If he wants to waste his time looking after pitiful little me, he can have at it. As long as he stays out of my way."

"What's that?" Lissa pointed to the paper, not liking the determined glint in her friend's eye.

"The address of a garage near the rail yard. One of the guys Javier hangs with at the center works there, and—"

"Maggie, you're not going over there by yourself?" Lissa reached for her arm. "That's crazy!"

"Is it crazy to want to keep a thirteen-year-old kid in school and out of jail?"

"It is, if you're doing it because you're really trying to save a girl who's been dead for almost eight years!"

Maggie jerked away.

Without another word, she jammed her cell phone into the pocket of her jeans, grabbed her keys and backpack and stormed out of the house.

Yep, Lissa was going to have to find herself a new nanny. But first, she was phoning the sheriff's department.

Tony needed to know what his niece was up to, even if it meant Lissa's new friend never spoke to her again.

"YOU'RE TELLING ME a war is inevitable?" Pineview's sheriff Dillon Reed rubbed at the base of his neck while Matt stretched the stiffness from his own.

They'd been at this through doughnuts for breakfast, sandwiches for lunch and more trips to the break room for reheated, stale coffee than Matt wanted to think about. First with Lewis and Rivers, then Sheriff Reed had joined them a little over an hour ago. Now it was after five and everyone in the conference room was ready to call it a day.

He was desperate for a few hours' sleep before he headed back over to the Wilmington place and…

And what? Watched from the shadows all night, hoping Maggie would take another moonlit walk? Or did he have the balls to actually ring the doorbell and insist that she let him back in?

"The war's already started," Matt explained, shoving aside what might happen tonight. What was going on now was too important. "I know you want to hear about gang prevention, but containment is your concern. The rail yard was just the first battle. You've got an entrenched Latino gang that's been fed over the last few years by a steady stream of legal and illegal immigrants moving into the area. Now there's an African-American set in Pineview showing their colors. You said kids are getting roughed up in the schools, pressured to pick sides. The graffiti I've seen is all about turf and dominance. There'll be strategic hits to secure position. Your gang activity is no longer confined to neighborhoods and communities."

"Meaning?" Lewis asked.

"Maybe some key players transferred from one county high school to another. Or a deal went sour, or was busted by a rival. It doesn't matter how it started. Control is in play, and the violence is only going to escalate until we get the leaders together and find a compromise that'll stop it."

"And the heavy recruiting?" Sheriff Reed asked. "Both gangs are expanding faster than ever before."

"When you're going to war, size matters. You'll see kids being given less and less of a choice, like this student of Maggie's. They ask nicely at first, but that doesn't last long. Eventually, they stop asking."

"And you think our increase in armed robberies is linked, too?" Tony asked.

"War takes dollars. And there's an intimidation factor. A gang has to dominate. The community has to know who's in charge. If you're not afraid enough of the thugs in your own backyard, you just might turn to the guys one backyard over for protection."

The two sheriffs exchanged stares. The last thing they wanted to hear was that the gangs were there to stay. If law enforcement tried to stomp them out overtly, they would just grow stronger. But if the cops did nothing, the situation would only get worse.

"How do we minimize the damage until we get this contained?" Reed asked.

Matt winced. "Get to know the culture. Each gang is different, even if they're part of a larger national group. Your men have to get to know the members. Their graffiti, their tats and their monikers. You'll want to have informants on the inside, and those kinds of relationships can take months, years to build. The more experienced the officers working on your gang cases, the better. But you'll need some of them to jump in as soon as possible, to see what they can do. There's a lot of risk involved, but a handful of deputies dedicated to containment can make a real difference, while the rest of your force catches up."

"You're talking about a unit like yours in New York." Lewis looked as if he were already sifting through a mental roster of his officers.

"As many of your deputies as you can spare should specialize. Guys, and women, too, if you have them, who aren't intimidated by the violence of the lifestyle. They'll be working non-traditional hours. Understanding the guns and the drugs is a given. And they'll have to be good at dealing with people, not just out to crush criminal behavior. It's a fine line to walk, but your officers have to want to help the gang members out of the cycle they've created, not just bring them down."

The very fine line Matt had stopped being able to walk with his own team.

The line he'd begun to walk again since coming to *Nowhere,* Georgia. He'd gone into this kind of work not just because he was good at it. He cared, damn it, and coming here to help Maggie had given him the chance to remember that.

"The things you're talking about will take funding and community support," Lewis said. "And that takes time. What can be done now, while we're waiting for the red tape to clear?"

Matt felt himself fully committing to the responsibility he'd taken only half-seriously until now. Two communities were being threatened. He could help do something about that.

"Long-term, you have to get into the schools and communities and keep at-risk youth from joining the gangs in the first place. They need other clubs to spend time with—recreational activities, organized by trained coordinators—that will fill the gap."

"Like Maggie does in New York?" Tony asked.

Matt nodded. "Short-term, pass emergency ordinances to crack down on some of the behavior that feeds the gang mentality. Up the penalties and fines for loitering, vandalism and disturbing the peace—especially in or near schools. Try to mediate the conflict that's already brewing. Intervene any way you constructively can. Investigate whatever crimes have already occurred, but prosecute individual gang members only when you have no other recourse. You have to pick your battles, which means cutting deals sometimes and offering immunity when it gives you leverage. Whatever it takes to earn your officers what little credibility and trust they can get. If the gang leaders think you're out for blood, they're going to treat you the same as they do their rivals. Finding ways to work with them isn't easy. It's not what your community's going to want to see at first. But challenge these gangs at every turn, and you become part of the war."

"Who do we know who's already got an in with these groups?" Reed asked.

"Some of our deputies volunteer at the youth center when they have free afternoons," Lewis offered.

"Several of the Latino kids we've known for years have recently started sporting gang colors," Tony added. "We can approach them, maybe try and get a meeting going."

"I'll see what kind of contacts my deputies have in Pineview," Reed added. "Some of the faces involved in recent drug busts have been a shock. Kids who used to be intramural basketball stars are circulating in and out of my jail like it's their own personal hangout."

"A joint effort is best from the start." Matt had already talked the idea through with Tony and Martin. "Make a list from both your forces of officers who're in a position to participate, then pool the names and contacts they cultivate. You'll need a point person from each county, maybe others for high-risk areas like clusters of low-income housing, affected schools and the youth center for sure."

"Tony?" Lewis asked. "This niece of yours. If

she's already working with this kid, Rodriguez, at the center—"

"No!" Tony and Matt responded in unison.

No way in hell!

Captain Lewis scowled.

"She's already pushed too hard to help a kid we think is being initiated," Tony explained. "Enough of our men work at the youth center. We'll find another way to make local contact."

"But if she has special training and understands how to work with hard-case kids—"

"Chief?" a deputy interrupted, popping his head in the door. "I have an urgent call for you. Line three."

Tony picked up the conference room phone.

"Maggie Rivers is close to one of the kids we want to target," Sheriff Lewis insisted. "Even if we have to keep her under departmental protection, we need—"

"Shit!" Tony slammed down the phone. In a heartbeat, he was already halfway to the door. "Lebretti, we're out of here. Maggie's gone after Rodriguez."

MAGGIE KNEW SHE SHOULDN'T have stormed out on Lissa like that. She should be back at the mansion, sifting through more paperwork, not parked outside what looked like an abandoned garage in one of the rattiest parts of Oakwood, thinking she was a rough teenager's last hope.

Like she'd once tried to be Claire's.

Had things really gone so far, she'd lost the line between the past and the present? Or was she just looking for an excuse to chicken out of this harebrained scheme?

If she bailed on Javier now, he was gone. No one else would come looking for him, including the aunt who'd been raising him since his mother spilt.

"He's never been nothin' but trouble," the woman had complained over the phone. "I got four more of my own, but they manage to keep their asses in school and out of trouble so teachers and social workers and parole officers aren't harassing me to be a better parent. I'm doing the best I can. If you're so worried about the little bastard, you hunt him down. I'm through with all this shit!"

That any adult, even someone who was *just* a legal guardian, could be through with a child never failed to piss Maggie off. Javier didn't believe there was anyone who'd stand by him, besides the gang of criminals he'd set his sights on. How could she stop trying to fix that while she had the chance?

She'd accomplished a lot over the weekend. She wasn't ready to make final designations from the trust or sign away the house, but she was dealing with the reality of it. Finally. And that tiny step forward had felt amazing.

So had making a few calls to try and locate her wayward student. It was the right thing to do. This wasn't about Claire or anything else. This was about facing what she had to do, instead of running from it. It was about not quitting, and being able to live with herself again.

She watched several older teens cross the street and slip around to the side door of the shop. Javier's friend, Alec, from the youth center was one of them. Most all the kids called him Joker. He sported a comedy-and-tragedy tattoo riding high on his chest, actually wrapping around the left side of his neck, with the number *13* woven around the masks.

His black clothing, the rosary beads he wore as a belt, it all fit. He couldn't be twenty yet, but Maggie had seen enough gang leaders to spot the type. And Javier had supposedly been trailing after him for years. If Joker was here, there was a good chance Javier would be, too.

She was safe enough waiting in the truck with the doors locked. Javier would have to come out eventually. And when he did, she'd find a way to talk with him one last time.

She settled back, resting her head against the seat, and wrapped her shaking hands around the truck's steering wheel. Not quitting and not being terrified were two different things. But she could freak out about what she was doing later.

Wham!

The truck shook with the force of something hitting the roof.

A shadow outside her window rushed closer, followed by the sound of shattering glass as something struck the side of the truck. Screaming, she dropped to the floor and covered her head. The pounding continued, beating away at the metal that protected her.

The windshield exploded next.

"Oh, my God." Terrified, Maggie patted the floor beneath the passenger seat. She'd dropped her cell phone. If she could just find it.

The battered driver's door was yanked open and hands wrapped around her ankles.

"Oh, God!"

"Get out here, you nosey bitch," a disembodied voice grated. "I've got what you're looking for."

"No!" She kicked backward.

She strained toward the passenger door and her only chance of escape.

One final kick, followed by an angry grunt, and Maggie was free. She scrambled to her knees and was reaching for the door handle when that window imploded. A jagged chunk of glass raked her cheek. The bastard behind her grabbed her leg again. A hand reached inside the window above her head and flipped the lock.

The passenger door opened to the sound of wrenching metal, and suddenly she was staring into Joker's eyes.

"You son of a bitch!" she yelled, still kicking at whoever was holding her from behind. "What have you done with Javier?"

Joker sneered in the silence that suddenly filled the truck. He lifted the bat he'd rested on his shoulder and pointed behind her.

"Why don't you ask him yourself?"

She swung her head around to find Javier the owner of the hands restraining her legs.

"What—"

"Get the hell off of her!" a blessedly familiar voice boomed from nearby.

"Sheriff's department!" someone else shouted.

Then, amidst the sound of curses and sneakers

scrambling on pavement, pain suddenly swamped the right side of her head, pinwheels bursting behind her eyes as she crumpled to the floor.

CHAPTER ELEVEN

"YOU'RE GOING TO do what?" Lissa couldn't believe her ears.

Martin hadn't stopped by that morning. Instead, he'd come over after dinner. The girls were bathed and ready for bed. They were curled up in her room watching cartoons. Lissa hadn't seen any harm in inviting Martin in.

What else was there to do with her night, besides balancing the monthly budget that was forever teetering closer and closer to the red, even with her full-time job and the child support Chris paid every six weeks?

Yeah, avoiding her woeful finances was the reason she'd handed the man sitting beside her on the couch a glass of wine instead of their customary coffee.

She liked Martin. A lot. Maybe a lot more than she'd been ready to admit. He clearly liked something about her, too, if Saturday was any indication.

But five minutes of listening to what Sheriff Lewis was planning for him and Tony had ruined her taste for her wine, and her wistful fantasy that Martin had stopped by to pick up where they'd left off at the movies.

"We're going to start by meeting with the leaders of the two rival gangs in some neutral place," he explained. "Next week, hopefully, if Tony can get the approval from Lewis and the Pineview sheriff. I talked with him and Lebretti before my shift ended. They were still at it in the conference room when I left. It'll be dangerous work, and…" He flushed. "I felt like I owed you a heads-up. I'm not exactly sure why, since we haven't agreed to, you know…"

"Be more than…" She gestured between them, when she couldn't find the right words, either.

"Yeah." Those eyes that normally teased grew serious, then slumberous in a way that shot straight through her worry about how risky his job was about to become. "But you have to know I'd like it to be more…whenever you're ready. *If* you're ever ready. And I didn't want to get deeper into working with the gangs without… I thought you should know. What you think about it would be important to me if we…if things got more serious."

What she thought was important to him?

Was there anything about Martin that would turn out to be what she'd expected?

"I…I don't want anything to happen to you," she admitted.

There was more to it than that, of course. But they were only supposed to be friends enjoying a healthy bit of summer fun. Anything more just…

Just what?

And she'd been lecturing *Maggie* on not wanting to face the truth.

"I didn't expect this, either, Lissa." Martin moved closer, all strength and rough gentleness, in that easy way of his that made her feel safe and cherished. Never threatened, though he towered over her. Never taken for granted, because she was the center of his attention whenever they were together. "But after all these years, I think I've finally found someone I'd like to be important to. I know a lot of women are happy keeping things casual with me because of the hours I keep. Not to mention the danger cops face. And as much as I like hearing that you care, I'll understand—"

"My sister was on the force, Martin. She almost died several years ago, remember?" Lissa shrugged off the memory of waiting at the hospital with her parents, wondering if Angie was going to make it after taking a bullet protecting Tony and Maggie from a drug dealer who'd already killed twice. "I know what you do for a living."

"Yeah, well, in the past it hasn't been all that much," he admitted.

He'd hadn't exactly been the most gung-ho member of the sheriff's department until the last few years. But everyone in town had noticed the shift in his priorities, due in no small part to Tony's influence. He'd matured, after being forever the local wild child. It was one of the first things that had caught Lissa's attention, the times they'd run into each other at her sister's. Then, after her disastrous divorce, and after Martin had made his shoulder more and more available for her to lean on, he'd captured her interest completely.

Compared to her ex, he was the slow, sweet, Southern Prince Charming she'd never thought she'd find.

"You're a fine cop. I know Tony depends on you. Sam Lewis, too." She laid a tentative hand on his arm. Stared at his chest, cringing at her reluctance to take the initiative with a man for the first time in her life. "And you're a wonderful guy. If working with this team the sheriff's forming with Pineview is what you think you have to do, then do it. I'll find a way to live with the rest, if…"

"If we end up doing more than ignoring movies together?" His finger lifted her chin. He smiled at the unsteady breath she took. "If we're talking about what I want, then you have to know it's you, Lissa. It's probably too soon for you to believe that, and I'm the wrong man for you in just about every way I can think of. But…"

"But?" Memories of their kisses made her ache for more.

How wrong could something be that felt so amazing?

"But I've been watching Matt Lebretti worry over Maggie. And that got me thinking. What if you were the one in danger, or one of your girls? And just the thought of someone coming after you was enough to tell me one thing for certain. Good idea or not, I'd do just about anything to make sure you and your family are okay. You've gotten under my skin, Lissa Carter, and I'd be happy for you to stay there for as long as you can stand it."

She'd never heard caring for someone described with such simple words.

Dating Martin would be fun, she'd told Angie.

And being with him could never be dull or boring. But from the start, there'd been more to her feelings for him than she'd been willing to accept. She'd told herself she was just looking to have a good time. He was offering her so much more.

Which was it going to be? Reaching for what she really wanted, or playing it safe again?

"Lissa?" The brush of Martin's rough palm against her cheek sent delicious sensations scattering. His thumb gently rubbed at her temple. "What are you thinking in there?"

Thinking?

Breathing was difficult with him so close.

But her sigh felt so natural. And the way he inched closer, his bad-boy smile melting through her, seemed more natural still.

"I'm thinking about staying right where I am for a while." She turned until her knee was nestled between his. She ran her hands up the hard muscles covering the chest that was so not like her slender, marathon-running ex's, that her mouth watered every time she brushed up against him. "And that if this is how wanting what's wrong for me feels, then I've definitely been hung up on the *right* things for way too long."

The next thing she knew, her wrong man was kissing her.

Shoving aside worries about Maggie, or what Martin and Tony were getting themselves into with the gangs, not wasting another second wondering about what was right or wrong for her, she simply focused on feeling. Wrapping her arms around Martin's shoulders, losing herself in the taste and texture of his kisses, she followed her own advice and let herself fall.

Things might end messy. She might be real sorry, real soon. But what she felt in Martin's arms was worth the risk.

She had worked free all but one of the buttons on his uniform shirt, she'd just discovered a sensitive spot just below his rib cage that made him shiver, when his cell phone began ringing. He tensed, his fingers sliding from the tangle they were making of her hair.

"I'm sorry," he mumbled. His lips grazed her cheek as he drew away. "Just let me… It's a 911 from Tony."

She stiffened at the anxiety in his tone.

"This is Martin," he said into the phone. "What's up?"

Their eyes locked. His widened.

"Holy shit! I'll meet you there." He flipped the phone closed and shot to his feet. His hand grabbed hers as she stood, too. “Maggie’s been hurt. Tony and Lebretti are on their way to the ER with her now.”

“WE NEED WHATEVER details she can give us,” a man said just outside the Emergency Room alcove Maggie had been rolled into. “Now, Rivers.”

“She’s not talking to anyone yet,” Tony insisted. “She has a mild concussion, she’s barely awake and she’s terrified.”

Maggie groaned as another wave of nausea consumed her. She slid farther beneath the lightweight blanket, wishing she could slither away completely.

She’d come to in the truck, only seconds after passing out. Matt had been cradling her, holding something to the gash on the side of her face. The rest of the last two hours had been a blur of ambulance sirens and her heart racing, as her mind sucked in every sight and sound on its mission to torment her.

Now, the aftershocks of the worst panic attack she’d ever had were making it excruciating to be near anyone, even the professionals trying to look after her. Finally alone in her corner, she was trying desperately to pull herself together.

Javier had tried to hurt her, just as Matt had predicted he would. And she'd served herself up to him on a silver platter. Then she'd capitalized on her stupidity by completely falling apart in front of everyone.

All the care she'd put into helping a kid who hated her for her efforts, all the pains she'd taken to prevent her family from seeing how truly screwed up she was, and for what? She could have saved herself and everyone else a ton of trouble by just giving up on Javier from the start, and wearing every emotional hang-up she had on her sleeve.

"The doctor said she was going to be fine," the other man insisted.

"Fine!" Tony replied. "If Lebretti and I hadn't gotten there when we did, she'd be dealing with a hell of a lot more than a blow to the head."

"But she's not, and we need information. You said you recognized a few faces, but we've got no one to interrogate."

"No one's going anywhere near Maggie right now," Matt countered.

He'd held her while she was weak and shaking, until the ambulance arrived. And she needed to be back in his arms so badly right now, it took her biting her lip to keep from calling his name.

If he touched her, she'd go to pieces again.

"She didn't just happen across our boys," he continued. "They must have seen her outside the garage and decided to make an example of her."

"Exactly why she needs to be interviewed," said the man who must be the new sheriff who'd replaced Angie. "The MS-13s are becoming bolder. They're a threat to everyone in this community. If she knows—"

"*She's* out of this, as of now," Matt insisted.

"Detective, this is *my* department's investigation. I appreciate your insight, but this is really none of your concern. I—"

"Everything that affects Maggie Rivers is my concern!"

"Matt—" Tony cautioned. "Why don't we take a walk—"

"I'm not going anywhere. Not until I see Maggie. Not until I'm sure these bastards stay the hell away from her."

"Son." Maggie could picture the sheriff squaring off against Matt. "I don't know how you boys conduct yourself in New York, but no one talks to me like that around here."

"Then I guess it's a good thing I don't work for you, isn't it?"

"Lebretti," Tony interceded again.

"Way I hear it," the sheriff continued over his chief, sweet Southern charm dripping from each word, "you're not exactly working back home, either. Something about an anger-management problem that's sidelined you, and might just keep you there for good."

"That's right." Scuffling followed Matt's response. He was losing control.

"Lebretti!" Tony bit out over the sound of something hitting the wall outside her curtained alcove.

The shouts…the violence…it was closing in again… Too close… Too much…

"I've got nothing to lose, *Sheriff*." Matt made the title sound like a curse. "So understand that I'm dead serious when I say Maggie's had enough. No one else, nothing else, is going to upset her. You got it?"

She struggled to sit up, one hand clutching at the blanket that covered the whisper-thin gown she wore. The other braced her pounding head so it wouldn't fall off her shoulders

"Tony?" she called out so weakly there was no way the angry men in the hall could hear.

But the argument outside stilled. Tony stepped through the curtain, his glare for the men he left behind warming to concern as he stepped toward her bed.

"How you doing, Maggs?" It was his forever-ago name for her. The result was devastating.

When she covered her mouth to muffle a sob, Tony reached to hug her. Panic at the thought of his hands, anyone's hands but Matt's, touching her, had her yanking away with a cry that shamed her to her toes.

This was what she'd been afraid of most. Who she didn't want to be.

"Darlin'?" he soothed, his arms dropping to his side. "It's going to be okay."

She couldn't stop the hysterical laugh that escaped at his word choice, any more than she could keep herself from flinching when he reached for her again.

"Maggie?" He held his hands up. "I know those creeps scared you, but it's okay—"

"It's not!" she insisted, the unfamiliar, scratchy voice coming from somewhere deep. A place that had stayed hidden for years, the walls cracking under the pressure, until the violence of the gang's attack had been the fatal blow.

She'd been hiding it for so long. Eight years of ignoring the trauma she'd willfully refused to face, just so it could all come crashing down around her now.

Good plan, Maggie!

"Nothing's okay." She could only manage a whisper this time.

She could see Claire's blood staining her hands again. It had been everywhere. She could still hear the shot that had smashed into the wall near them, and remember how Claire's killer had locked the same gun on Maggie, a second before the man's head exploded when Tony killed him.

Then there were Javier and Joker's hands on her. She'd been defenseless, her greatest fear, and this time no one had been there to save her.

"God, make it stop!"

"Maggie?" Tony sounded ready to cry himself, and suddenly mad as hell. "For God's sake! I know you want to do this on your own, and that you need your space, but that space almost got you killed tonight. You trusted me once before, darlin', when you were just a kid. Trust me just one more time, honey. Come home and let Angie and me help you sort this out. Please."

Her head jerked up from where she'd buried it in her hands. The room spun, along with her stomach, but it was the reality that she needed help, that she'd needed it for years, that made her the sickest. She couldn't launch herself into her uncle's strong arms, no matter how much she needed to, because she wouldn't be able to tolerate being touched until the panic faded completely.

"You want to help me sort things out?" From somewhere, she called up the strength to stand, when what her body wanted was to sink back into the bed. "Get me out of here, then leave me the hell alone."

Maybe alone *was* the only way she could handle anything anymore.

So be it.

"Maggie, the doctors want to—"

"You said I was fine, I heard you." She wasn't, of course, but when had that mattered? "I want out of here, and I don't care how many people I have to fight to do it. Either help me, or get out of my way."

She let the blanket drop to the floor, ignored the hand he reached to help her and somehow managed to shuffle toward the chair her clothes had been draped over.

"Maggie, you're not walking out of here alone. Not until we catch Javier and whoever else hurt you. Sheriff Lewis wants your statement as soon as you can give it. You can't just—"

"I..." She gripped the back of the chair and weathered a fresh batch of nausea. "I can't be here. I'll give you my statement. I'll stay at my great-grandfather's house with the alarm on. Post as many men outside as you think you need to. Just please, get me out of here, Tony. Please."

She'd begged him for help when she'd been a scared kid. She prayed his inability to deny her anything was just as strong now.

"What about Matt?" he asked.

"What?" The clothes slipped through her shaking fingers. "No!"

"He's right outside, and he wants—"

"No! I can't."

She'd never get her emotions under control with Matt around. One more of those compassionate, pitying looks that saw too much, and it would be game over.

She needed to salvage something of who she thought she was, before she lost herself completely.

"Maggie—"

"No! Matt's the last person I want near me."

CHAPTER TWELVE

"I'M NOT GOING anywhere, lady," Matt warned Nina through the half-open front door of the Wilmington mansion. "Not until I see her for myself. Either let me in, or step back."

He'd knock the door down if he had to.

Matt's the last person I want near me.

Maggie had known he was in the ER. She'd gone out of her way not to look at him when she left with Tony—against doctor's orders. But she'd meant for Matt to hear her parting shot.

She'd never wanted anyone to see her like this, him most of all. She hated that he'd been the one holding her at the garage.

Well, she could beat away at him all she wanted, but she wasn't shoving him aside this time.

"Give her some space," Martin Rhodes had said as he'd blocked Matt from following Maggie and her uncle out of the hospital.

Not a chance.

Exactly what he'd said to Tony when the man had returned home at two in the morning, after helping Maggie settle in at the mansion, then getting the boot for his troubles. Tony had wanted Matt to wait at least until the sun was up before trying to see her. Maggie's parents were flying in later that day. The Rivers family was closing ranks.

Which meant Matt only had a few hours to get through to Maggie.

He'd almost lost something very precious tonight. Something he couldn't stop his heart from wanting, even if he was crazy to think he could have it.

Maggie.

His fury at the punks who'd hurt her suddenly turned inward, at the target that deserved it most. If he'd realized how much she meant to him while they were in New York, if he'd bridged the distance between them then, instead of being almost grateful for it, she might have stayed and gotten the help she needed.

And this might never have happened.

"I love her," he heard himself say to the scowling housekeeper. The fact that he was speaking the words to a stranger, when he'd never had the guts to say them to Maggie, made him even more of an asshole. "I know she doesn't want to see anyone, but she can't keep trying to handle this on her own. Let me in. Let me help her."

The elderly woman loosened her death grip on the door.

"She's been up all night wandering around this place," Nina said. "I don't think what's haunting her in here is any easier to bear than those punks she's trying to keep locked out there. If you've come to make trouble—"

"All I want is to love her, if I can."

To see her. Hold her again. To somehow convince himself that it wasn't too late to finally try and be what she needed him to be.

The local sheriffs needed him, too. The cache of weapons they'd found in the back of the body shop had confirmed Matt's suspicions. The MS-13s were stockpiling for all-out war. He had a job to do—one he'd been all set to dive back into full-time, because that was what he did best.

Then Maggie had driven up to that garage unarmed. Alone. And his priorities had never been more clear.

"She's got to let someone help her." He was pleading with a woman he barely knew. "She's done this alone long enough."

Nodding slowly, her eyes shrewdly assessing, Nina stepped out of his way.

"Thank you."

"Don't thank me," the elderly woman countered as he walked by. "Just help her. You cause her any more pain, and I'll call one of the gardeners up here to kick your butt back out of this house."

MAGGIE OLIVIA RIVERS.

Maggie pushed back from her great-grandfather's desk and stood, needing distance from the real estate contract she'd finally worked up the nerve to sign. In the middle of the night… Under cover of darkness… But she'd signed it.

Way to face up to reality, champ!

The offer from the private girls' school was ready for the lawyers to work their magic. Every line the broker had marked with a tab was now graced with either initials or a signature. A whole new generation of girls would fall in love with the Wilmington mansion's turn-of-the-century architecture and painstakingly manicured grounds.

She was finally freed from watching the place rot away unused, and from hating herself for not being able to let it go. If only she could be free of the rest of it.

Everyone who mattered to her would know the truth soon. There was no hiding it, not after her display at the garage and the hospital. Tony had no doubt called her parents. There'd be nowhere to hide once they arrived. Anticipating the shock and disappointment on her family's faces had her head hurting even worse.

So did knowing that she was more disappointed in herself than they ever could be.

"Why aren't you in bed?" a deep voice asked.

Maggie jumped backward so quickly, she was certain she'd left her aching head behind. She made a grab for the swivel chair, only to gasp as it shifted on its rollers. Her balance took an inconvenient hike, but she was saved from kissing the hardwood at her feet when strong arms closed around her waist, pulling her to an even stronger body.

"I got you." Matt eased her back into the chair, his touch as devastating as it was gentle.

"Don't." She shrank away.

Not because she was afraid, as she had been each time Tony had tried to comfort her.

With Matt, she only wanted to get closer, and that was worse.

"Then get in bed like the doctor wanted," he responded as he moved out of reach.

His touch had been almost clinical, same as his words. The other night's emotion was firmly in check.

Then their gazes collided. Concern and worry swirled in his too-blue eyes.

"Get away from me, Matt." She sounded terrified, because she was. But not for the reasons he obviously thought as he moved back several more feet.

As if him being on the other side of the room would be enough to keep her from wanting to throw herself into his arms and beg him to never go back to a world she couldn't be a part of.

"I'll keep my distance," he reasoned gently. "But I'm not leaving. You need to start taking care of yourself, or you're going back to the hospital. Tony agrees with me. So does Nina, or she'd never have let me through the front door."

"Thank you for your concern." She didn't sound the least bit thankful, but that was too damn bad. "I had some paperwork to finish up, then I was heading upstairs. So go back to my uncle and tell him that all is well. Your obligation here is fulfilled."

Matt's eyes narrowed.

"The doctor insisted someone wake you every three or four hours tonight, to keep an eye on the concussion. How is that going to happen, if you won't let anyone close enough to check on you?"

"Doesn't matter." The longer he stood there

like a desperate dream come true, the harder it was to believe she didn't need him. "I'm not sleeping, so why keep someone up all night worrying about me? It's just a bump on the head."

"You were unconscious, Maggie!"

"For a whole thirty seconds!"

"You've had the scare of your life."

"Trust me, I've been scared worse."

Matt inhaled.

"You couldn't even stand on your own two feet when I came in here," he added in a softer tone that hurt her head more than if he'd yelled.

It was a familiar cause and effect. Matt got concerned. She got scared. She wanted him to hold her. Then she ran from the truth that she'd always need him, whether she liked it or not.

"You startled me, and I stumbled." To prove her point, she pushed to her feet and stood her ground, even when she could have sworn the floor shifted beneath her. Then the pounding in her head decided her stomach needed to join in the fun. Or maybe it was the shock of the last four hours finally crashing down on her, now that she had an audience to enjoy her misery.

"Oh, God." Slapping a hand over her mouth, she raced to the bathroom that adjoined the study.

She braced herself against every stick of furniture she passed, then the wall, determined not to give her rubbery knees the satisfaction of depositing her on her backside. Matt was right behind her as she made it to the dimness of the room, a split second before she sank to the floor and threw up in the toilet.

Matt brushed her hair away from her face, his nearness as he knelt behind her as comforting to her suddenly chilled body as a warm blanket. She wanted to melt into him. But she didn't dare let herself.

"Just lean against me for a minute," he murmured when the worst had passed. Pulling her closer despite her resistance, he curved his body around hers. "I'm not going anywhere, Maggie, so stop fighting me. I don't care if you want help or not, I'm staying tonight for as long as you need me."

I'm staying…for as long as you need me.

And suddenly, even if he couldn't possibly mean what he'd promised, the loneliness was too much. There, on her knees, in the arms of the man she'd sworn never to need again, she lost the ability to run one more time.

She turned toward him as the floodgates opened. Flashes of Javier and Joker's sneering faces attacked. They were reaching for her, intent on hurting her. She could hear them laughing as she fought. Feel Javier's brutal grip. Then the sound became the deafening ring of gunfire, and it was Claire's pale face she was seeing. Her killer's sneer as he turned the weapon on Maggie. The final showdown had happened behind the mansion, in the overseer's cottage, and Tony had almost been shot protecting her…Angie had almost died….

Clapping her hands over her ears, she felt the scream rising from somewhere deeper than the memories.

"Maggie!" Matt held her even tighter. "Maggie? Baby, what is it?

"They were going to k-kill me." The strong woman she'd so wanted to be for him evaporated. "They were g-going to—"

"Shh…" Matt's body was solid beneath the cheek that now rested on his chest. But his touch on her hair as he pressed her even closer, his lips as they kissed the top of her head, and his voice, had never been softer. "No one's ever going to hurt you again. No more. You're going to get through this, you're going to face whatever you have to then you're going to be safe, damn it. This ends now!"

She whimpered against his chest. Breathed in

his familiar, clean scent. Let the dark hint of spice that always clung to him overwhelm the memories. There was so much to face. Too much. But not yet. For now, for this moment, there was only Matt.

When she'd quieted, he tilted her head back and gazed into her eyes.

"The doctor said your pupils would be dilated, and you'd be nauseated if you were having trouble with the concussion," he explained. "Your vision okay?"

She nodded, why he'd come hitting home all over again. *The doctor said.* She'd been injured. She was broken. He felt a responsibility to fix her problems, like he'd fixed so many other people's on the job.

"I'm okay now." She tried to get up, tried to move away, but she couldn't make her body cooperate. "I just have to take it a little slower for a while."

He flushed the toilet and lowered the lid, helping her up until she could sit. His hand never left her shoulder as he filled a cup with water and handed it over.

"Drink this." Moving away finally, leaving her biting her lip at the loss of contact, he rummaged through the cabinet below the sink and produced a small bottle of mouthwash. "And some of this."

He added a splash of the minty liquid to her

cup and stood back, but not too far, as she got up. She swished a watered-down mouthful and spit into the sink.

The burst of freshness tasted like heaven.

"Thank you."

"Let's get you to bed." He cupped her elbow and led her back into the study.

"I…I don't want to sleep." She shuddered as they reached the hall and started toward the spiraling staircase. "I tried. All I do is remember, and I can't…I don't want to remember anymore tonight."

She wanted to forget so badly, she'd just signed away this house and any future she might have had here.

"Then you'll just rest." Going up and down the stairs alone had been agony. With Matt's shoulder to lean on, it wasn't nearly as bad. "I'll sit with you. We can talk. I'll hold you if…if you think that would help."

He sounded as rattled as she felt.

They reached the upper landing, and then her bedroom. He was helping her ease onto the bed, and still she hadn't decided if she wanted him to stay. As if there was any doubt that she needed him there, even when it was bound to end badly for both of them. It was what she'd craved since he'd shown up in town.

Matt finally understanding. Being willing to accept what she hadn't wanted to. Not leaving her to face everything alone. Matt being there, when she couldn't stand to be with anyone else.

She linked her fingers with his and tugged until he sat beside her. "I don't know if... You have to have so many questions, work to do with Tony's department..."

"Everything else can wait." His hand cupped her cheek, his thumb pressing against her lips. When her breath caught against the pressure, he seemed to stop breathing, too. "Just let me be here for you tonight, the way I should have tried to be in New York."

"You didn't know." She hated the guilt in his eyes.

"I should have realized there was more to what you were going through," he argued. "I should have asked. You're a good actress, Maggie. But you're not that good. Your family had no idea how much of the past you were carrying around inside you. But I could see you were hurting, and all I could think about was how it would affect my work."

"You—"

"I'm a selfish bastard." His stare dropped to her lips, and his head moved a few inches closer, then he jerked away, cursing. "I wanted you with no strings attached. Then when things got rough, when the strings tightened, I let you go without a fight. I told myself the job was more important."

"If you're so selfish, what are you doing in Oakwood?" He'd been nothing but careful and gentle since he'd shown up on her doorstep. There was so much inside him that he refused to see. "Why are you here babysitting me tonight?"

"I'm trying like hell to be the kind of friend I should have been to you all along." His voice hardened with the same urgency that was chipping away at her control. And still, his words were tender, and the contrast was the most erotic thing she'd ever heard.

"Maybe...maybe I don't want any more friends," she stuttered.

Hadn't she been bracing herself to finally deal with the truth? The truth was that what she craved, dangerous or not, was Matt. The way he'd been before things fell apart, the way *they'd* been when they'd first met. Lost and free and unaware of anything more than the magic waiting for them every time they were in each other's arms.

Just once more.

"Maggie—"

Her kiss silenced him. She swallowed his hungry growl. Tasted him with her tongue. Ran trembling fingers up the muscles of his stomach until she could smooth them over his ribs.

He gripped her shoulders. Drew her closer, the friction of his chest pressing against hers causing her to cry out, only this time from the need for more instead of her toxic memories.

“Is this what you want, Maggie?” he asked against her lips, his slow, sweet kiss teasing at the truth she’d tried to bury. “Whatever you want, anything, it’s yours. But be sure.”

Anything. Everything. He could be it all. At least for tonight.

She’d pushed him away, every way she knew how. But he’d followed her, first to Oakwood, then back to the mansion, night after night. And she’d held him off, so certain she was doing the right thing for both of them.

The only thing she was sure of now was that she couldn’t push him away anymore.

“I…I need you.” She leaned deeper into his touch. “I need—”

She lost the rest in his kiss, the raw sound he made as his lips covered hers. His hands were as strong as she remembered, his touch magic. He stroked her back, then around to her breasts. He filled his palms with her as his mouth left a trail of kisses on its way to her ear.

"I don't want to hurt you." His words were both a caress and a warning.

She arched closer and let her own hands explore. Knowing he needed her, hard and demanding, even as his hands soothed down her back, the only thing that could hurt now was if he stopped.

"Then love me," she whispered.

She tensed, waiting for him to start edging away, same as he always had when things got too real. But he eased her back into the mattress instead, his strong body covering her.

She closed her eyes. Fought the memories that were still so tangled with her emotions.

"Shh," Matt murmured again. His fingers slid beneath the hem of her top to flick across the navel ring he loved to play with. "Don't think, Maggie. Just feel. Let me make it better."

His mouth took over, freeing his hands to work at the fastenings of her drawstring pants. Cool, midnight-black hair filled her hands when she reached for him, tugging his head closer as pleasure consumed her.

Her clothes disappeared beneath his touch.

"Matt, please," she begged.

"I'm right here, baby." His mouth dipped lower still. "I'm not going anywhere."

Clutching at the bedspread beneath her, she let herself go. Let his gentleness and the hard promise in his voice sweep her away. This was for her. He couldn't have made it clearer. For the first time, he was focused solely on her, open and giving, yet just as driven to control the incredible things he made her feel.

God help them both when it was finally time to wake up from this dream. It would be her biggest screw-up yet. But just this once, she was grabbing what she wanted, no matter the risks.

CHAPTER THIRTEEN

"WHERE IS SHE?" Eric demanded as soon as he and Carrinne made it into the terminal where Tony had met Maggie a little over a month ago. "She's not answering her cell."

"Maggie's at her great-grandfather's place." Tony's quick call to his brother last evening was all it had taken.

Eric and Carrinne had always respected Maggie's independence. But their daughter's recklessness and refusal to ask for help when she needed it had reached the point where she was a danger to herself. Eric and Carrinne had caught the first flight they could out of Manhattan, and after a five-hour layover had made a predawn connection on the regional airline that serviced Oakwood.

"Two of my men are stationed outside the mansion," Tony reassured them. "No one's getting by them."

"You'll drop us off on your way back to the station?" Carrinne looked worse than her husband.

"Yeah, but—"

"I have to see her. I don't care how early it is."

"I know, but—"

"Tony, what is it?" Eric laid a hand on his wife's shoulder to silence her reply. Tough as nails and always ready for a crisis, he looked one shock away from coming completely unglued. No man could love a child more than Eric did the daughter he'd only known for ten years. "What aren't you telling us?"

"It's just that right now might not be a good time to barge in over there."

"You said Maggie hasn't been sleeping. That she won't let anyone stay with her, even though she checked herself out of the hospital early."

"Yeah, well, that's the thing." Tony had actually been relieved when one of his deputies phoned with the news. His brother, no matter how realistic he was about his little girl being all grown up, probably wasn't going to share Tony's relief. "Maggie's not exactly alone anymore...."

MATT PULLED the sleeping woman in his arms closer, his hand never stopping its sweeping caress over the soft skin beneath his fingers.

Maggie was mesmerizing. Tough and sweet and smart and vulnerable. A deadly combination for a man who'd been starved for all of it ever since she'd left him.

He was going to have to wake her soon. The doctor had warned that there was still a risk of complications. Someone should periodically wake her up and check her pupil reflexes. And Matt had promised Tony he'd call if he wasn't able to get in and do just that.

Well, he'd gotten in.

Back into a relationship the woman in his arms was certain he didn't want. She was still terrified of so much more than the MS-13s…being with him most of all. His world was too hard for someone with her history. She didn't feel safe with him, because when she'd first run, he'd let her go.

Now, nothing mattered but talking her out of running again. When she'd lost control, she'd begged him to love her. And, God help them both, he did. He always would.

Maggie stiffened in his arms, just a slight movement, but it was enough to tell him she was awake. Yet she didn't open her eyes. Her mind was no doubt already consumed with regret over what they'd done, everything they'd said.

"Don't even think about it," he murmured against her hair. His arms tightened around her. "Don't think about how to escape from me again, Maggie. Don't think about yesterday or anything else. Just lie here and let me hold you."

Meaning something to this woman, being there until she decided what would make her whole again. Nothing had ever meant more. Not even the job that had been his life for so long, he hadn't known who he was without it. Until now.

He could find a way to live without being a cop. But living without Maggie…

She was trembling, fighting against the weakness she was so sure would disappoint everyone. Didn't she know she was *his* hero? Yes, she was beautiful and smart. But she also had a strength that humbled him, the kind of courage a man could build his life around.

"For a second—" she lifted her head and brushed dark curls from her eyes "—I thought I'd dreamed you up."

Despite the confusion and shadows still lingering in her eyes, he chuckled.

"I'm not sure I'd call last night a dream." Kissing her softly, when everything else about him was growing harder by the second, felt damn good. "A fantasy, maybe."

"Yeah." She snuggled closer, wreaking havoc on his good intentions. "That part was amazing. It always is. But I mean…you know, you wanting to stay, even…wanting to talk…"

"We should have talked a long time ago." He turned until their foreheads touched and he could intertwine their fingers. "I made myself believe we didn't have to. Then things kept getting worse, and I didn't think I could. But…" He stopped to clear his throat.

"*I* couldn't talk about it." She ducked her head. "Why do you think I made it all about your job, when—"

"You were hurting, Maggie. And I was the reason."

"No!" Her eyes rose back to his. "No, you were showing me what I wanted. What I needed. But I couldn't love you and not be afraid, and if I gave in to my fear, I couldn't hide from the rest. Which meant I couldn't have you. What…what kind of coward gives up like that? Just packs up and runs, instead of dealing with…with all of it."

His breathing stilled. He could have sworn he felt his heart stop beating in his chest.

"Does that mean you're ready to deal with it now?" He sounded like the desperate man he was.

Her reaction was immediate.

She inched away and sat up. Holding the sheet around her with one hand, she shoved more of her hair out of her face.

"I'm so screwed up," she said on a bitter laugh. "I've got my family in an uproar. The local police are wasting precious resources protecting me, because I kept putting myself in danger but refused to see it. And now you, of all people, are pitying me."

He took her shoulders and gently pulled her back to the mound of feather-soft pillows.

"You must have hurt your head worse than that doctor said, if you think what we just did was about pity."

She'd started softening beneath his touch when the sound of footsteps coming up the mahogany staircase startled them both.

"Maggie!" a man called.

"Oh, my God," Maggie squeaked at the same moment the bedroom door few open.

"Get out of here, Lebretti!" Eric Rivers demanded. "My daughter's avoided you for months, but now that she's too weak to throw you out, you think it's a fine time to make your move?"

Tony had entered a step behind Maggie's father, and he didn't look much happier. But he did seem less ready to knock Matt's teeth down his throat.

Matt edged toward the center of the bed, hiding as much of Maggie from view as possible.

"Captain Rivers," he said. "Give me a minute to get dressed, and we can talk downstairs."

"Oh, you're getting dressed," Eric agreed smoothly. "Then you're getting the hell out of this house!"

"You're the one who needs to leave, Dad. Matt's here because I want him to be." Maggie swung her legs over the edge of the bed as she clutched the sheet to her chest. On a different woman, the gesture might have made her look guilty. Maggie, however, was pissed. "In sixty seconds, if you're still standing there glowering at Matt, you're going to get more of an eyeful than you already have. And that's a family moment I think we all can live without."

"Maggie—"

"Give us a minute, Captain." Matt took Maggie's hand, part of him needing the contact. But he also wanted her family to understand, wanted Maggie to understand, that he wasn't going anywhere. "We'll be downstairs soon."

"Come on, Eric." Tony turned his now-unresisting brother toward the door and pushed. His backward glance was for Maggie alone. "Sorry. I tried to keep them away."

"Them?" Maggie stalled in the process of

trying to toe a discarded gym sock from under the bed.

"Your mom's downstairs." His glance flickered to Matt. "Don't take too long."

The door shut behind them.

Maggie's shoulders slumped.

"I knew this was coming," she said in a whisper.

"What?" Matt slipped into his jeans and knelt in front of her.

"My parents." She gestured toward the door. "No way were they going to sit this out in New York. They'll stay until they know every last detail."

"Know what, Maggie? What's so terrible you don't think the rest of us can handle it? That you've been hurt? That you've been in pain for years, and no one tried hard enough to help you?"

She grabbed for his hands. He'd never get used to her reaching for him, after he'd been so sure she never would again.

"How hard it's been every day," she continued, hanging her head. "How much of the last year I've just wanted to quit."

"Quit?"

"I'm a quitter, Matt. I want to quit my family and this person I'm pretending to be. I want to quit school and my job, because nothing fits anymore, no matter how much I try to make it. I quit *you* after Bill's death, because you saw too much, and that was getting too difficult. I want to *quit* everything!"

"You've been through a lot." The loathing in her voice was unbearable. "And you've handled it better than anyone could have. Look at me. I've trashed my career because I couldn't deal with my partner dying, not to mention losing too many battles with gang hoods half my age who see killing and destroying their neighborhoods as just another way to do business. You were eighteen years old when Claire was shot. You lost your best friend."

"But you dealt with it, Matt. You went after Flores until you got him. It was a mistake, but at least you didn't…"

"Didn't what?" He needed to know, and she had to realize that he could handle the truth, whatever it was.

That he'd be right there beside her, refusing to let her shut down, no matter what she said. No matter what happened with her family downstairs.

"I didn't what?" he repeated.

"You never wanted to…to end it." And then the strongest woman he'd ever known dissolved into his arms and held on for dear life. "And sometimes

I do. That's why I agreed to see that doctor. But it didn't work. Talking to her just made things worse, until I couldn't stand it. I would have done anything to stop feeling that way."

"So you ran?" Thank God, because the alternative she was describing was unthinkable.

Maggie nodded against his chest.

"Matt… Sometimes I want it all to go away so badly, it…it scares me."

CHAPTER FOURTEEN

"MARTIN WAS AT THE STATION most of the night." Lissa and her sister were sitting together on the ancient swing that dominated Angie's screened-in porch.

Sarah was asleep beside them in her own swing, and Lissa's girls had Garret out playing in the backyard sandbox while the temperature was still cool. She'd called in sick to the bank. There was too much going on with the people she cared about to be able to focus on anything else today.

It was a lovely, sunny Oakwood morning. Too bad the threat of gang violence was a sea of brooding darkness, waiting to spill into the everyday lives being lived in backyards all over town. Even after all her sister and brother-in-law had said over the last few months, she'd had no idea things would get so dangerous so quickly.

What if Lissa hadn't called to warn Tony yesterday afternoon? Maggie could have been killed.

And it sounded like things were about to get even worse for Oakwood's deputies.

"How serious is it?" she asked Angie, knowing she had no right, but she couldn't seem to help it. "What does Lewis have planned?"

Her sister's marriage to Oakwood's chief deputy gave her access to all kind of departmental information. But Angie never talked about cases, and Lissa had never had any reason to ask.

Now she did.

Lissa didn't want to think of Martin helping lead the charge to stop the kind of violence that had touched Maggie yesterday. In too short a period of time, he had become important to her. He was honest and fun and more than a little bit wild. And if that simple honesty hadn't gotten to her, the way he clearly cared about the people in his life would have.

Once one of the baddest of the bad boys in town, he'd been shaken by the news of Maggie's attack, not only when he'd left Lissa to head for the scene, but also when he'd called later with the details. She'd heard his heart in his words, as well as his determination to find and stop the scum responsible before anyone else got hurt. She'd never been prouder to know him, or more worried about the risks he and Tony and the other deputies took.

"Lissa." A smile played across Angie's face as Garret giggled. Callie and Meagan were dumping buckets of sand over his head. "You know I can't—"

"I think I've fallen in love with Martin," Lissa closed her eyes against the answering shock on her sister's face. "I don't know, maybe it's just—"

"Sex?" Angie sputtered.

"No! We haven't slept together yet. Not that I… I mean, I think we will, as soon as we…"

As soon as we can string ten minutes alone together?

Great. Sounding desperate for sex. A perfect way to get Angie to take her seriously.

"What happened to all of that unattached fun you were looking forward to having?" her sister asked.

"I care about him." Much more than should be possible. "Callie and Meagan will, too, once they spend more time with him. But I know things are heating up with the local gangs. Everyone in town's talking about how the department's cracking down after what happened over at the rail yard. And now that Maggie's been attacked… I don't want to put Martin on the spot, but…"

"But you have no problem asking *me* questions I shouldn't be answering."

Angie continued to rock the swing she'd received from their mother as a wedding gift. The two of them had spent entire days on this thing as children, enduring the summer heat on their parents' porch. Swinging and talking, reading, playing. It hadn't mattered what they did, as long as they were together. The youngest of five sisters, they had a special bond that had seen them through a lot. The broken engagement that had crushed Angie only months after the realization that she'd never be able to have children of her own. Angie and Tony's crazy courtship years later, a relationship Lissa had fought from the beginning, until she'd seen that Tony was the perfect match for her strong-willed, sensitive big sister. The gunshot wound that had almost taken Angie from all of them, Chris's affair and then her divorce.

She couldn't remember a time when she and Angie hadn't been there for one another, offering the rare bond of support and love that only sisters understood.

And Lissa needed that support now.

"I never expected to care about Martin like this," she admitted in the silence of the shady porch. "Not this quickly. I know he's doing what he has to for the job. For the community. And if

I'm going to spend more time with him, I'll have to accept the risks he takes. But not knowing what's going on is… It's…"

"It's hard for all the wives and girlfriends." Angie's by-the-book stare was that of the former top law enforcement officer in the county.

But she'd broken more than a few regulations in her day, most of them to protect the man she'd built her life around. Angie breathed a near-silent curse and turned in the swing to face her.

"The few tidbits of information they've collected are telling the department that an all-out war is brewing between the gang here and a rival one in Pineview. Matt Lebretti's been pushing the importance of the two departments working together. Tony and Sam Lewis have to worry about containing the violence now, before it gets worse and more people are hurt."

Lissa listened with growing horror. Like most of her friends and neighbors, she'd always felt sheltered here in this close-knit Southern community. They'd had their scares, but issues like drugs and gangs and guns and women being beaten in their cars were big-city problems she'd never thought she'd have to worry about.

"What… What does containing the violence mean exactly?" Whatever Tony decided, she had no doubt Martin would be right there, covering his friend's back.

"If I had to guess?" It didn't sound like Angie was guessing one bit. "They'll go after one of the gang headquarters, either MS-13s here or the Pineview group, whichever location they can pinpoint first. And when they do, things are going to get tricky."

People were going to be hurt. Maybe even die.

Lissa could see the truth in the harsh lines of her sister's face. It was time for the sheriffs' departments to take a stand. The gangs weren't in charge anymore. And Martin and Tony would be right in the thick of it.

Lissa checked her watch, stunned to find that it was already after noon. Martin had said he'd be at the station most of the morning, but he was hoping to catch a few hours of sleep in the afternoon before he and Tony were due back for their late shift tonight. Glancing at the kids happily playing in her sister's yard, remembering the pain on Maggie's face while she talked herself out of caring for the man who was so obviously her match in every way that mattered, Lissa made up her mind.

"Would you mind watching the girls this afternoon?" she asked.

Angie's sharp look softened into a shrewd smile that tilted up one corner of her mouth.

"Errands to run?" she asked.

"No."

"Brought too much work home, and the girls would be a distraction?"

"No!" Getting angry was pointless, but why couldn't her sister give *I told you so* a rest just this once?

"You need to be alone, so you and the laundry can develop a more meaningful relationship?"

"Angie!" Her girls looked up at her exasperated tone. "Knock it off. I just need a few hours to…"

Jump Martin Rhodes?

"To meet up with a friend?" The teasing was gone from her sister's voice. Her eyes were full to brimming with both tears and understanding.

"Yeah." Lissa wiped at the corner of her own eye. "A really good friend I don't think knows just how much he means to me."

"That's what I figured." Her sister nodded, watching the kids get back to their sandcastles. Her watery chuckle was vintage Angie. "Probably why I already told Tony that Callie and Meagan would be staying for dinner."

She'd known. Even before Lissa had, she'd already guessed what the latest gang developments would do to Lissa's waffling anxiety over taking the next step with the first man she'd wanted to be with since Chris. Martin had probably said something to Tony about Saturday, and Tony had mentioned it to his wife. And Angie had pieced the truth together out of almost nothing. She'd always been good at that.

She'd known the whole damn time.

"You're an ass," Lissa said, starting to chuckle herself.

"Yeah," Angie agreed. "But you love me anyway."

"Lord knows, I do."

Just a year after the devastating end of her marriage, she'd been lucky enough to find a man she could care about again. And she didn't know who was more excited by her chance for a new start, her or her pain-in-the-butt sister.

"I NEED TO TALK to Mom alone," Maggie said.

She and Matt found her family, along with Nina, milling around in the kitchen. Everyone had a cup of coffee in their hands, or steaming on the table or counter in front of them. They looked dug in for as long as it took to get the goods on her screwed-up life.

There wouldn't be more than five minutes of explanation. She wasn't the brave woman she'd wanted to believe she was. She never had been.

Even now, she couldn't do this in front of all of them. She wasn't even sure how to face her mom.

"This concerns all of us, Maggie." Her father's patience was gone, but the rock-solid love she'd never doubted was still there, softening the hard lines of his face.

"Yeah, I've made this everyone's problem. And you all deserve the truth, but I…"

Matt's arm wrapped around her from behind, and she leaned into his strength. Clung to the reality that he was still there. That for once, she'd faced what *she* hadn't wanted to see in herself, and he'd been there the whole time, holding her and accepting what she still couldn't. As if she could trust him until she found a way to trust herself again.

The way she should have trusted her family in the first place.

"I can't face all of you, and say what I have to say. I…I just can't do it."

Both her uncle's and her father's frowns deepened. She doubted either of them had ever heard the word *can't* come out of her mouth. She braced herself for their disappointment. Their realization that the woman they'd been so proud of had never existed.

Then her father stood and wrapped her in his arms as Matt let go.

"You talk to your mother, darlin'." He tucked her head beneath his chin. "We'll still be here when you're done."

She silently sobbed against his chest, breathing becoming even more difficult as she felt him flinch, then hold on tighter.

"It's going to be okay," he insisted, repeating Matt's promise with the same ring of determination. "You don't have to be anything but okay, Maggie. We'll figure out the rest. We'll all be here for you for as long as it takes."

Nodding, wiping at her eyes with the back of her hand, she edged away. Glancing up, she caught her dad and Matt measuring each other with equally arrogant stares. Then she turned to her mom, leaving the men in her family to get comfortable with Matt's precarious place in her life, when she wasn't even certain what that was.

But dream or not, she needed him to be there when she came back. And, God help her, she was starting to believe that he would be.

"Come on." Her mother held out her hand. "Let's talk."

"WHEN...WHEN DID IT START?" Maggie's mom asked in a strangled whisper.

They'd moved to the privacy of the solarium.

But the warm, quiet room they both loved wasn't a haven for either of them at the moment. She'd just revealed her New York's therapist's concern that for several months before her treatment began, she'd been unconsciously trying to hurt herself.

"Christmastime." About six months after she moved in with Matt. Six months after coming back here for Oliver's funeral, and the nightmares and flashbacks had begun.

At first she'd ignored them as merely inconvenient. She'd moved on from the past. She'd created a wonderful life for herself. She was something of a marvel, considering how quickly she'd gotten over the shock and the grief. At least that's what everyone had told her. Who was she to argue?

"Post-traumatic stress disorder?" Her mother's forehead wrinkled as she absorbed more of Maggie's story.

"Something like it." It was fairly common, and not that complicated to understand once Maggie searched the term on the Internet. "I know it sounds far-fetched. I didn't want to believe it, either. But the fact is, I never dealt with my feelings when everything went so wrong with Claire. Losing her, almost being killed myself. It was easier to go on. Live my life. I told myself I wasn't going to give up on my dreams of college and teaching."

"It was too easy." Her mom's voice suddenly sounded far away. "Lissa said something like that to Angie when you first came back here. That you were handling things too well and something was off. Angie assumed her sister was just picking up on your breakup with Detective Lebretti."

"Matt was part of it." A big part of her desperation to get away, before it became impossible to hide her problem, from herself most of all. "But this has been coming for years."

"And none of us knew." Guilt mingled with her mother's confusion. "I mean we knew, but we had no idea how much you were hurting. How could we not have seen this? How could we not have gotten you the help you needed when you were a teenager?"

"Because *I* didn't want to see it, Mom!" If either one of them started crying that would be it. "The doctor said something about me being stuck in the denial phase of grief. That I was avoiding facing what had happened, even though I kept subconsciously putting myself in situations that forced me to deal with all of it. But I ignored her. This isn't about you or Dad or anyone else not seeing the truth. This is about *me,* and how useless

I've become, all because I refused to face the truth. Being your perfect daughter, the perfect teacher and the perfect girlfriend sounded like a lot more fun, so I ran with it. But I guess my mind knew better. Inside, I was as screwed up as ever, just like the doctor said I would be if I didn't slow down and deal with what I had to. The school figured it out first. It was only a matter of time before the rest of you did."

Her mother's expression went from weepy to flat-out angry in record time.

"Is that what this quack has been telling you?" she demanded. "That you're a screwup, because you have feelings? The same useless twit who never bothered to get you any help, or tell anyone else what you were going through?"

"I didn't want help, Mom! Because that would have meant I had a problem. There was nothing wrong with me. I was… I was just…falling down stairs and driving through red lights. I had a list of perfectly logical explanations for every accident. The doctor suggested there could be more to it than that, but I wouldn't listen. I'm the one who did this, not the doctor. *I'm* the one who wanted…"

Her voice had risen to a shout. A table of budding camellias confronted her when she turned away. Their cheery blossoms smiled at her scowl, taunting her with the reminder of the simple summer days she'd once spent planting lovely things all over the grounds she'd just sold to new owners.

An angry kick to the base of the table, and it and the plants went flying. She hadn't realized she'd screamed, until the shrill sound pierced the dregs of the headache still loitering behind her eyes.

"You wanted what, Maggie?" Her mom looked crazy scared.

"I wanted…"

She'd wanted it to be over. She'd wanted out.

"What does it matter what I want?" she ranted on. "I want this place, but everything here hurts so damn much I just signed it all away." A low shelf of baby ferns were the next to bear the brunt of her rage. "Having what I want would have meant facing what I've become and dealing with it, one way or another. But I'm a coward, Mom, and a quitter. I've run for so long, I don't know how to do anything else."

"You're not running now." Misguided pride shone in her mother's eyes. "And you're not a coward."

"Of course I am. Don't you get it? I wasn't pretending for you. I was pretending for *me.*" She'd taken the easy way out. "I wanted to be what everyone else expected me to be. I didn't want to admit that I…I just couldn't. And now it's all gone. My work in New York, my chance to stop a kid who's more damaged than Claire ever was. My life with Matt. And now you guys have come all the way down here, when there's nothing you can do."

"That's not true," Matt said from the door of the solarium. His chest rose and fell heavily with each breath. He must have heard the commotion and come running. Her dad and Tony filled the doorway behind him.

They were all there now, seeing who she really was, and the mess she'd never wanted anyone to know about.

"There's plenty that can be done," her mom agreed calmly. "Now that we know what's going on, we'll find you a better doctor. One that specializes in delayed stress disorders. You'll take all the time you need. The job, the schoolwork, it can all wait until you're ready. And don't go telling me I don't understand. I've been where you are. I almost gave up everything, rather than reaching for the life I have with you and your dad, remember?"

Of course Maggie remembered. She recalled every bitter fight she'd had with her mother about the donor surgery that had almost never happened. She hadn't been able to understand how someone as strong as her mother could be dying, or how she wouldn't initially allow Maggie to take whatever risks were necessary to save her life. Her mother had been afraid, and she'd been running scared, and Maggie had called her a coward.

"But eventually, I learned to let you and your dad in." Her mom walked to Matt's side. The woman who'd been her first hero, standing in solidarity with the man who was the one dream Maggie hadn't been able to give up on, so she'd thrown him away instead. "And now it's time you did the same."

"I…" Her mother's quiet acceptance was like a new world opening up.

A world that had been there all along, only Maggie had been too afraid to believe in it. The loved ones, including Matt, that were circling around her didn't care what was wrong, as long as she let them help. As long as she was willing to fight to get better.

Behind Matt and her mom, her dad and Tony stood like a wall of protection, refusing to let her believe anything but that they cared, and they always would.

"I'm so sorry. I...I tried." She clenched her hands against the frustration and rage and failure still churning inside her. "I wanted...I wanted to be as strong as the rest of you...."

"You're doing just fine," Matt responded.

"Pretty damn great, considering," Tony chimed in.

Her dad stepped past her mother and reached for Maggie's hand. It was hard to tell who was more relieved that she didn't shy away, her or him. It was as if, now that her family knew everything, her mind no longer saw them as a threat.

"You've been a miracle to me from the first moment I learned about you, Maggie." Ten years ago, she'd walked up to him like they were in some Dr. Seuss rhyme, and she'd known instantly that he was her father. "Every day of my life is now perfect, darlin', just because you're there. You don't have to pretend to be anything for me. Ever. You can't scare any of us off. Whatever you have to do to get better, we're behind you one hundred percent."

She held on to her father as she gazed at her family and Matt. Their expressions ranged from accepting to fiercely determined. Nowhere was the shock or disappointment she'd dreaded for so long.

"The doctor was talking about clinical depression," she admitted. "Maybe an anxiety disorder triggered by the memories and delayed stress. Tendencies to…toward self-destructive behavior when I feel too close to losing control, because subconsciously I was trying to force things to fall apart my way, rather than waiting for bad things to happen to me."

"Like walking away from our apartment that night?" Matt asked.

"Or hunting down Javier, when you knew there was nothing more you could do?" Tony added.

"Or agreeing to sell this place when you didn't want to," her mom said. "Because you couldn't face the memories here?"

They were reciting her various mistakes as if they were discussing a problem with the weather. They had her back—ugly, un-Rivers-like emotions and all.

"Yeah." She eased from her father's grasp. "And I've kind of done a number on my job."

She'd picked one of the most dangerous schools in Manhattan to work in, just to prove to herself she could handle it. Clearly, she couldn't.

"That's fixable." Her dad's hands settled into his back pockets—his thinking stance. "The school system's damn lucky to have someone as intelligent and talented as you teaching their high-risk kids. Once you've worked through this, they'd be crazy not to want you back." He paused, as if struck by an unfamiliar thought. "If… If that's what *you* want. If not, you'll be great at whatever you decide to do next."

His unconditional support shamed her all over again. When had she decided to trust the fear more than she had her family or herself?

"I…I don't know what I want to do," she admitted.

Choosing honesty over covering up her confusion felt unbelievably good.

"Then don't do anything for a while, darlin'." Her father's wink had always been the most amazing thing. Seeing it now, she felt the first honest-to-God smile in ages spread across her own face. "There's no rush. Nothing you need to do but get better."

Matt had said the exact same thing to her that morning. He, like Lissa, had been so certain her family would be behind her, helping her, as soon as she was ready to talk to them. And there he stood now, right beside them, in this sunny room that suddenly felt more like home than anything had in a long time.

She smiled at his knowing expression.

Could she and Matt really build something out of everything she'd destroyed?

The cell phone she'd slipped into the pocket of her jeans chose that moment to ring, piercing the quiet that had taken hold after her dad's final words. Pulling it out with every intention of sending the caller to voice mail, she glanced at the display and froze.

"Maggie?" Matt stepped closer. "What is it?"

She dropped the phone.

"It's Javier," she said in a strangled whisper. "I gave him my number, in…in case he ever needed help between our tutoring appointments."

"Javier?" Her father's protective hug enclosed her in a pocket of safety between him and Matt.

"The boy she's been helping at the youth center," Matt explained.

"And one of the assholes who attacked her yesterday."

The phone kept ringing as Matt picked it up. A few more times, and it would roll to the message service.

"I should answer it," she said weakly, knowing what she had to do, but unable to reach for the device. "He…he might really be calling for help. What if he's changed his mind?"

It rang again.

"Or, he and his posse might be ready to take a second crack at you, and he's calling to set up the hit." Matt's voice was coldly furious, the same tone as when he'd talked about the ambush that had taken his partner's life.

"Give me the phone." She reached, but he pulled it farther away.

"It's a trap, Maggie." His voice was softer now, pleading. "There's nothing you can do for him, except get yourself hurt again."

Another ring.

"Give me the phone, and we'll know for sure, won't we?" If she copped out, if she ran again and she was wrong, she'd never be able to live with herself. "You're all behind me, whatever I have to do, remember? Then give me the phone, and let's finish this."

CHAPTER FIFTEEN

"LISSA!" Martin was shirtless and dripping in sweat.

Lissa's first thought was, *Yum.*

He doesn't exactly look thrilled to see you on his doorstep in the middle of the day, was thought number two.

"I...I'll come back another time." She was already turning to go. *Let's get it on* suddenly didn't seem like such a bright idea.

She'd stopped by home on the way over, to freshen up and put on the sole *come and get me* halter top she possessed. She'd traded her shorts for the low-rise jeans that hugged her hips and hit her tummy at just the right place to flatten what tended to pouch.

She wasn't sex on a stick, but she looked pretty good for thirty-two. Alluring in a wholesome way. Martin had been chasing her for months. How hard could this be?

Pretty hard, evidently, when a woman was

shaking in her buy-one-get-one-free discount sandals.

"Wait!" He grabbed her elbow. Lord, he smelled good. Sweaty and earthy, with the musk of his cologne still strong enough to hint at how amazing he'd be shower-fresh. "I'm trashed because I was working out. I just got back from the station and didn't know how long I had, so I hit my free weights before I headed in for a nap. If you don't mind waiting, I'll wash up and be right out. Where are the girls?"

"At my sister's." Lissa followed him inside, holding back the comment that a sweaty, half-naked man with bulging muscles was her definition of perfect, not trashed. "I knew you'd be busy following up on what happened to Maggie. But I thought, maybe..."

He grabbed a towel from the back of what looked like a Stickley lounge chair.

"Maybe what?" It was hard to tell what distracted her more, the way his tongue licked at the corner of his mouth as he smiled, or the room full of carved, classic oak furniture.

"Are these antiques?" She ran a loving hand over the sideboard he was using as a low table behind his couch.

"My parents were big collectors." He shrugged.

"They're both gone now. Keeping all this feels a little like having them around still."

The history that enveloped antique furniture had always fascinated her. The romance and the beauty of owning something timeless made her long to shop flea markets and tag sales to find pieces of her own. But Chris had balked at buying someone else's castoffs. He hadn't even wanted the few pieces her family had offered when they'd married. His tastes had run toward the clean, metallic lines of the contemporary fare touted in almost every showroom nowadays.

But rough, tough, one-of-the-boys Martin was sentimental about his parents' things. He had a heart that wouldn't quit. And he was currently watching her stare with her mouth gaping.

"Maybe, what?" His eyes gleamed with something much hotter than sentiment.

"What?" How was she supposed to convince her mouth to shut when he was running a hand down his damp chest.

"The kids are at your sister's, so you thought, maybe…"

"I…I was free, so I thought we could continue our…discussion from Saturday."

He stepped closer and the room faded away. The world shrunk. Everything else closed in on the tiny space the two of them now occupied—this amazing man, and everything she could see herself wanting with him.

"You mean what we were doing during the movie?" He slipped her purse from her shoulder and dropped it to the priceless coffee table. He inched closer, as if to kiss her, then changed direction. Brushing his lips across her cheek, he kept going until he could whisper in her ear. "I'm afraid I still need that shower, so another…discussion…will have to wait. Unless…"

"U-unless?" His fingers were busy with her halter-top ties.

The rasp of his knuckles against the sensitive skin of her neck called up a little squeak of surprise before she could stop the sound.

Appalled at her blushing-virgin response, determined to show Martin that she craved this as much as he did, she lifted her hair to make his task easier. But when the ties finally gave way and the loose ends began to trail downwards, she grabbed at the material still covering her chest.

She wanted him. He wanted her. This should be as simple as physiological chemistry got. A nice diversion.

And suddenly *not* going to happen.

Not this way.

She didn't doubt that they could have a mind-blowing afternoon of delight, but she needed more. He'd talked like he did, too, but was he sure?

She'd once dreamed of happily-ever-afters and believed that's the way love would always turn out. Now, not being certain what the man she was dreaming about wanted was an indulgence she and her girls couldn't afford.

"Lissa?" He ran soothing fingers up and down her arm. "You're not going to break my heart and make me take that shower all by myself, are you?"

"Your…your heart?"

"It's yours, honey, if you want it. I know it sounds crazy coming from a guy like me. But I love you, Lissa. You gonna let me show you how much?"

Weakened by the tremor in his voice, she let the fabric slide from her fingers. To the casual observer, Martin might be nowhere near as right for her as her refined, conservative ex.

But in her eyes, he was perfect.

"I…I think…I don't know how… But, I think I love you, too," she said on a gasp as his hands began smoothing her top down her body.

Her fingers tangled in the damp hair covering his chest. His hands found her breasts as his lips lowered, his growl of appreciation joining her sigh. Stretching on her toes, she was just beginning to lose herself in the most perfect kiss of her life, when a distant beeping had the overheating man in her arms stiffening, and not in the way a revved-up woman wanted.

Panting, Martin pulled back, his eyes stormy with passion and regret.

"I'm sorry, I have to—" He turned to the table behind him and grabbed his cell phone.

"I understand."

Even if she didn't want to.

She *wanted* to be in the shower running her soapy fingers over that body she'd been lusting over for months. But every officer in two counties was most likely on call at the moment, Martin most of all, given how closely he and Tony worked together.

He pecked a brief kiss on her lips and flipped open the phone to check the display. She began pulling her clothes back together as it rang again.

"It's Tony." He punched the button to answer the call. "Something must be up."

"I TOLD JAVIER to call back later tonight," Maggie explained to the crowd assembled in the conference room at the Oakwood Sheriff's Department. "That I needed time to think things through and get rid of my family. Just tell me what you want me to say next, and I'll do it."

She had the attention of every officer in the room, and Matt was no exception. Except unlike everyone else, Matt's mind wasn't on the information she could possibly score about the local gang's whereabouts.

He couldn't get past the courage she'd shown, standing up to her family. Facing the truth herself. Or the wonder in her eyes when everyone had backed her up, surrounding her with the support that for some reason she'd believed wouldn't be there. Now, still sporting a bruise on the left side of her face, she was staring down a situation that clearly terrified her.

She'd held it together when Javier had asked her to meet him, to *talk,* in a secluded storage unit down by the train station. And she hadn't taken no for an answer when she'd demanded to accompany Matt, her father and Tony to the sheriff's department for the meeting about their next move. She looked one surprise away from falling apart again, but she was determined not to run from what she thought she had to do—help stop the escalating violence in the community, and hopefully get Javier off the streets before he got himself killed.

"You have his cell number now," Sheriff Lewis said. "If he doesn't contact you again soon to set a time, we'll have you call him."

"I don't think that's a good idea," Matt got in a split second before her uncle and father's emphatic *nos*.

Lewis looked ready to throw the lot of them out and handle this on his own, if they didn't stop hovering like a pack of overprotective big brothers.

"You don't want her to appear to be pushing for the meeting," Matt reasoned. "Right now, she looks hesitant. If Javier's buddies get suspicious, the window of opportunity slams shut. If they want to make an example of her badly enough, the kid'll call. If she's the mark he has to bag to show his loyalty to his new brothers, we're in."

Maggie swallowed as if she might throw up again.

"I don't want my daughter anywhere near those bastards," Eric Rivers ground out.

"Who said anything about sending her in?" Lewis had tolerated the former sheriff's involvement so far, but his cutting glance announced just how thin his patience had stretched. "She gives us a time and a place, and we send in a double. It worked once before, didn't it?"

He was referring to the drug sting that Maggie had been mixed up in as a teenager. Matt had pulled the records as soon as he hit town. Carrinne had given him the high points, but he'd needed to know it all. Years ago, Maggie had royally pissed off Oakwood's first drug lord. Her uncle had set up a confrontation with the guy, using a double for Maggie as bait. Far from the text-book ending they'd hoped for, and despite the precautions they'd put in places, the operation had resulted in Maggie nearly being killed.

Matt suspected she was fending off memories of the ordeal now, as she rubbed her bruised temple.

"Maggie stays at the station the entire time," Tony insisted. "We're not taking any chances. She doesn't budge from this building until we bring down as many of the MS-13s as we can."

"Matt will be with me," Maggie added, double-checking with a glance his way. "I'll be fine here."

She was far from fine, but she was facing what terrified her. And she wanted Matt beside her while she did it. Maybe even for longer than that.

What he wouldn't give for a quiet, shadowy corner to pull her close and show her just how proud of he was of her.

Lewis scanned the grim expressions of the men grouped around the conference table, all of them ready to take a bullet for the woman who was bravely offering to step back into yesterday's nightmare.

"All right." He nodded. "Ms. Rivers takes the kid's call when it comes in, and she promises him whatever she has to for the hookup to happen. Tony." He turned to his chief. "Get your team together and pick another officer to help lead the team. Include the men from the Pineview department you and Dillon Reed discussed. Be quiet and be quick. I want those boys in custody before anyone else in town knows what's happening."

"Martin'll be my point." Tony glanced toward his friend, receiving a brief, affirmative nod in return. "We'll call the rest of the guys in, and we'll regroup once everyone's here. Should be ready to go within the hour."

Maggie stood watching it all in silence, still massaging the side of her head.

"Hang on to me, baby," Matt murmured into her hair as he wrapped his arm around her waist. "I'll be here every step of the way this time."

However close she wanted him, or however much space she required to keep it together, that's where he'd be.

As long as she understood that he wasn't losing her to the fear and the past all over again.

CHAPTER SIXTEEN

MAGGIE STEPPED OUT of the ladies' room and scanned the busy hallway for Matt. All afternoon, he'd never been more than a few feet away.

Javier hadn't called yet. She'd almost bailed on the plan at least a dozen times. But she kept finding a way to stay. Like splashing cold water on her face and taking a few minutes alone in the bathroom, to breathe without everyone watching her do it.

Her heart broke for the choices Javier had made, but he had to accept responsibility for his decisions. And Tony and his men were going to protect their community, because that's what heroes did.

Which brought her back to looking for Matt.

She recognized the sound of his voice coming from one of the smaller rooms down the hall, filtering through the milling crowd of officers waiting for word to either head to the scene, or back to their desks to provide whatever support would be required. She heard her father, too, as she approached the open door and stopped just outside.

"Your captain found out I was headed down here," her father said to Matt. "He phoned to ask if I'd relay a message. It seems you're not answering Sanders's calls or returning his voice mails."

"I'm on suspension," Matt replied. "And I've had my hands full. I figured being fired could wait until I got back to Manhattan."

He sounded so matter-of-fact. Where was the man who'd lived and breathed his job since the day she'd met him? As calm and reasonable as she'd ever heard him, Matt sounded satisfied with being exactly where he was—in Oakwood with her.

Tears sprang to her eyes. She turned away.

"Internal Affairs has cleared you, son," her father said, his news bringing Maggie to a stumbling halt. "There will be a formal reprimand inserted in your file, and they're talking about a year of probation. But it looks like you're greenlighted to go back to active duty as soon as your suspension's up and you're through with your work down here."

Edging closer to the door rather than away, she

forced down the panic. Matt would be leaving for New York once the MS-13 situation was contained.

He'd want to return to his task force as soon as he could. She'd known that the first day he'd shown up in town, and she'd known it when she'd made love with him last night. He belonged in Manhattan, doing the work, making a difference in so many lives. And at least for now, maybe for a long while, there was no way she could be there with him.

"I saw you with my daughter," her father said when Matt didn't respond. "Whatever happened between you two in New York, you seem…determined to help her now."

"Yes, sir." Matt dropped a report on the desk and stood taller. "I care about Maggie very much."

He hadn't said he loved her. Matt might never be able to say those words. But everything he'd done for her in the last few days shouted *love* louder than he ever could.

When she was alone again, when he was back where he belonged, she'd find a way for that to be enough.

"And your job on the force?" her dad asked. "It's important to you, too?"

"Yes, sir."

Matt must have sensed her standing there. His gaze slowly shifted to hers.

Her father's did, too. "Then I guess you have an important decision to make."

"Yes, sir," Matt agreed as she turned to go. "I…"

She left the rest of their conversation behind. Shut down the drive to cling and hope for more than what Matt had already given her.

Because of him she was reaching for the help she'd needed so badly. Whatever his decision, whatever *he* needed next, she was going to support him.

Even if it meant letting him go all over again.

"DAD OR I WILL CALL as soon as we know something, Mom." Maggie's mother and Lissa were hanging out with the kids at Angie and Tony's place, all of them waiting and worried. "I'm fine. I'll talk to you soon."

Maggie flipped her cell closed and glanced to where Matt was talking with the Oakwood and Pineview sheriffs. Tony's team, including several officers from Pineview, was on its way to the rendezvous Maggie had set up with Javier. Matt caught her gaze, and she made herself smile reassuringly. He didn't look convinced by her efforts, but he stayed where he was.

Where she'd asked him to be—doing his job. He'd tried to talk with her after his conversation with her dad, but she'd insisted he get back to work. There'd be time enough for him to break the bad news later.

Maybe by then, she might even mean it when she said she'd be okay without him.

"Mom's worried about how you're handling this." Her dad had posted himself beside her like a guard dog.

Matt looked their way again, as Tony reported over his com link that they were approaching the warehouse Javier was *hiding out* in. The kid had said he was afraid to go home after what had happened at the garage, and afraid to go back to the MS-13s.

"Mom's not the only one who's worried." Maggie gave herself a fifty-fifty shot of getting through this without another meltdown.

"Let me take you down the hall, honey," her father offered. She turned to find him staring at Matt.

"I'm fine right where I am." The determination in her words earned her a raised eyebrow.

"I wish you'd give yourself more time." He grimaced and ran a hand through dark hair that had begun to gray over the last few years. "Some distance from this kind of life wouldn't be a bad idea for a while."

Distance from messed-up kids? From the police officers who fought every day to help them? From the man who would take as good care of the people he protected in his job as he had of her since arriving in town?

"I'd rather be scared," she said, making sure Matt was listening, "than hiding. Facing what I'm afraid of is the only shot I have of getting back the life I want."

Matt had shown her how to believe that. And who knew? Once she was better and could return to her degree and job in New York, he might still be willing to give her another chance.

She couldn't think of anything she wanted more.

"We're in," Martin's voice said over the com link that had been routed to the conference room speaker phone. Matt turned the volume up. Bracing his hands on the table's edge, he glared at the speaker impatiently, as if he could will the gang members to be brought into custody without any trouble. "Tony and I are covering the rear. Baker, you set out front?"

Toby Baker was Dillon Reed's point man on the team. Two other Pineview deputies and Oakwood's Buddy Tyler completed the group now surrounding the warehouse.

"Roger that," Baker confirmed. "Waiting for your signal."

Static filled the air around them for what seemed like an eternity. Maggie's dad slipped an arm around her shoulders, as if he knew she was imagining the worst—Javier or one of the gang resisting, and the armed confrontation that would likely erupt.

"Go," Tony ordered, then silence reigned once more.

Once the men were in position, communications were supposed to terminate until the scene was contained. No news was good news. The officers would report only if there was a problem, or once they had everything under control.

Every second that ticked by was excruciating.

No one moved in the conference room. Matt and the two sheriffs never looked up from the speaker. Matt was like a statue, completely focused.

Maggie could almost feel him remembering another raid he'd helped orchestrate, and the officer who hadn't come out of it alive, no matter how by-the-book everything had gone. Just as she couldn't silence her own memories of long-ago gunfire and death.

She gritted her teeth at the chill that rushed through her, digging in her heels and handling it, just like Matt.

"You want to wait in Tony's office?" her father asked.

"No." She shook her head. But she let herself lean against him, absorbing his support and strength. "I need to be here."

A blast of static echoed through the room as a com link opened. Gunshots could be heard, flying from various directions.

"Man down," Martin Rhodes bellowed through the speaker. "Officer down, Dispatch. Damn it, it's Rivers. I'm going in to cover."

"Roger, got your back!" another voice confirmed.

"Get paramedics over there now!" Sheriff Lewis shouted to an officer hovering at his elbow.

The sound of more shots filled the conference room. Matt's knuckles went white as he gripped the edge of the table. Maggie covered her mouth with her hand.

"Give me a status, boys," Lewis bit out. "Where's Rivers? What's going on?"

The crackle of gunfire was his answer, followed by a grunt and a cry of agony.

"Freeze! Drop your weapon," an officer

demanded, his voice, even over the open com link, leaving no question of his intent. Whomever he was talking to either did as he was told, or the officer would fire.

But it wasn't Martin who'd spoken. And there'd been no word from Tony at all.

Maggie stumbled closer to the speaker, her dad's hands supporting her.

Why wasn't anyone saying anything?

More shots fired at close range.

"Site contained," an officer who still wasn't Martin finally reported. "Seven suspects, heavily armed."

"Do you need backup?" Dillon Reed asked into his own open feed.

"Negative, all weapons have been neutralized. But get medical over here now! Two officers down. One suspect. Repeat, two officers down, Rhodes and Rivers. Oh, God. It looks bad. Where's the damn ambulance?"

"On its way." Lewis made eye contact with Maggie and her dad. He rubbed a shaking hand across his jaw.

Matt was looking, too. Everyone in the room was. God only knew what they saw as they stared at her. She couldn't feel her expression. She couldn't feel any part of her body.

Feeling would have meant processing what she'd just heard.

Tony and Martin were hurt, both of them.

It looks bad.

"Maggie!" she heard Matt say from what seemed like too far away.

He sprinted toward her as the room faded to black.

CHAPTER SEVENTEEN

MATT SAT IN AN UGLY, designed-to-be-uncomfortable hospital chair. Beside him on an ER exam table, a silent Maggie waited for the nurse to return with her discharge papers.

She'd scared him to death, fainting in her father's arms back at the station. Even though she'd woken mere minutes later, Matt and Eric had convinced her to get checked out. She couldn't be too careful after her concussion. Besides, they were all headed for the ER, anyway.

Captain Rivers had phoned his family on the way, and he was sitting in the waiting area now with his wife, sister-in-law and Lissa Carter, along with a passel of kids. The fact that Rivers had so readily left Maggie in Matt's care had come as a bit of a shock, but Matt would take whatever alone time he could get with the woman sitting next to him.

Not that Maggie's empty stare had encouraged him to say a single word in the last half hour.

"I can't believe I made a scene back there," she finally muttered.

For a second, he had no idea what she was talking about.

"You mean fainting? You're recovering from a concussion, and—"

"And I distracted everyone, because I couldn't handle—"

"No one expects you to be able to handle shit like that, Maggie!" He yanked himself from the chair and stalked to the other side of the tiny, curtained cubicle. "You shouldn't have been in that room at all. There was a very real possibility things were going to go south, and you don't need that kind of shock right now."

But she'd stayed, to be sure her uncle was okay. Maybe even to be sure Matt was okay. And a part of him had needed her there, even though every second of the waiting and the reality of the outcome had been excruciating for her.

"Still no news?" She hadn't flinched once at his or her father's hushed conversation during the ride over.

He'd have preferred hysterics.

"Nothing yet." He'd seen her like this before, when she'd been cool as a cucumber after deciding to dump him and move out of their apartment. "Your uncle and Rhodes are both in the ER. No one knows anything more, except that the deputies at the scene protected Matt and Tony as best they could until the medics could get to them."

The raid had gone well. The deputies had contained a violent situation as effectively as any of Matt's officers in Manhattan.

Casualties were to be expected. There'd be more. There were always more. But the alternative was to let the gangs take over the community, and to watch other kids meet the same fate as Maggie's student. Not too long ago, Matt had resigned himself to the inevitable. He'd been so sure there was nothing anyone could do anymore to make a difference.

He couldn't have been more wrong. Maggie's uncle and his team were proof of that.

"What about Javier?" she asked.

Matt stepped to the edge of the bed. He didn't want to crowd her, didn't want to break the fragile hold she was keeping on her emotions. But he wanted, needed, to be close enough to help her process the truth.

"One of the deputies said Javier opened fire on your uncle. He took Martin down, too, knowing another officer had him in his sights. The deputy didn't have a choice but to shoot. It was like…"

"It was like he'd rather be dead than not make it with the gang."

And now he was.

Matt brought her hand to his lips.

"None of this is your fault," he said. The guilt she was feeling was pointless and destructive. He'd learned that one the hard way. "You were part of it, but you did everything you could to stop Javier."

"I didn't do anything but make the situation harder for everyone." When he tried to keep her from standing, she shot him a *go-to-hell* look and ignored his offered support. "Shouldn't you be with Lewis and Reed, helping them sort everything out?"

"I'm exactly where I need to be." Her anger was a promising sign, he reminded himself. He'd take pissed-off over the alternative any day.

"Yeah. I'm sure babysitting me is tops on your to-do list. Right up there with stopping more gang-related deaths and injuries." She stood. "Give it up, Matt. When you're done consulting here, you'll hop on your bike and head back to New York, and I'll still be here with my family trying to scrape a life together. You saw what just happened to me at the station. There's no point pretending we'd have a chance in hell of making a relationship work, even if I do make it back to Manhattan. Just go!"

He grabbed her arm, ignoring her attempt to pull away.

"Go?" he snapped. "I'm supposed to follow you down here, realize how much I love you, how much I want you in my life, then I'm supposed to just go back home and forget all about you?"

Her head snapped up. Her complexion paled even further.

"Don't say that." She punched his shoulder. "Don't you dare say that to me after..."

"After what?" he demanded. "After you couldn't handle hearing people you care about get shot? You're the only one who thinks you should be able to miraculously get over everything you've been through."

She shook her head, the tears he'd never be able to stomach filling her eyes.

"Maggie, let me love you, baby." He brushed away the pain trailing down her cheeks. "Let me be here for you while we do whatever it takes to make this work."

"Don't!" This time she was out of reach before he could stop her.

"Don't be here for you?" He stared at the way

her hands trembled as she brushed them through her hair. "Or don't love you?"

He'd never felt anything more powerful than the desire to make the world right for this woman. For them both. There was nothing he wouldn't do to make that happen.

And she was giving up. Running.

Again.

"I…I love you, too, Matt. But, look at me. If we try to do this again, you're going to wake up one day and realize you've made a mistake."

She loved him.

He'd belittled her for saying it during their last night together in New York. He'd been waiting to hear it again ever since.

"We can make this work." He couldn't lose her now.

"I should have been there for you today," she reasoned. "The least I could have done was not make things more difficult. I can't even imagine what it was like, listening to the crossfire after what you've just been through with Bill, and—"

"Yes, you can. You went through the same thing with Claire. It was all coming back, I could see that from across the room."

"You lost your partner last month. I lost a friend when I was a kid." Leave it to Maggie to make even a sniffle sound brave. "Can you believe I actually bought into that warm fuzzy scene in the solarium, and thought I was ready for something more challenging than a group hug?"

"You did just fine."

"I was terrified!"

"So was I!"

Her startled blink made him smile. Then she stepped closer and laid an *it's-over* palm over his heart, and he was certain he'd never smile again.

"I want to be with you so badly, Matt. But you're a cop, and that's never going to change. I'll try as hard as I can, but… But, I'm afraid I might never be ready…."

"Yeah." He let her words wash over him.

She was afraid, and she needed time. He was pushing her, when he'd sworn he wouldn't.

"I don't want to hurt you anymore." He covered her hand with his.

"I don't want to hurt you, either," she whispered against his lips, her kiss and her worry for him equally rare and precious.

He was trying to take care of her, and she was fighting just as hard to do what she thought was right. For *him.* He deepened the kiss. Held on tighter.

"We'll figure this out," he promised them both.

"I CAN'T BELIEVE we haven't heard anything," Lissa said as calmly as she could manage. Her girls were playing in the corner of the visitors' lounge, entertaining Angie and Tony's kids with the basket of toys they'd found. The majority of Oakwood's off-duty deputies were lurking in the hallway outside. "Why haven't we heard anything?"

Outwardly, her sister was infuriatingly calm. But Lissa knew better. Angie was about to crawl out of her skin, or chew off the last of her thumbnail, whichever vented the fear first.

"The nurse said the doctor would be out as soon as they knew something," Angie said around the tip of her thumb. She grimaced, stared at the jagged edge she'd created, and dropped her hand to her lap. "They're doing everything they can. Eric, are you sure none of the other officers can tell you anything more?"

Sounding more desperate than Lissa had ever heard her, Angie glanced toward the children. She wiped at her eyes when she looked back to her brother-in-law, begging for something to hold on to when it felt like everything was slipping away.

Or maybe that's what Lissa was feeling, and it was easier to believe she wasn't alone.

"Only that the paramedics had Tony and Martin stabilized at the scene." Eric's hand twitched beneath his wife's grasp. The man valued family above all else. Waiting on news was as hard for him as the rest of them. "Martin was awake when they were loaded on the ambulance, Tony wasn't."

Martin had been awake.

Being awake was good, right?

Another glance at her sister shut down Lissa's pep talk. Angie's agony over what could be happening to the man she loved was everything Lissa was feeling and then some. Angie and Tony had built a life together. Lissa and Martin had merely talked and tempted each other with more. They'd come close to taking things a whole lot further, but close didn't cut it. Except Lissa wanted more. She'd never been so sure of anything in her life.

As crazy as it seemed, she'd found something to build new dreams on, after her toxic divorce had killed the ones she'd lived off her entire life. Martin's smiles and laughter and enormous heart were now part of the new start she'd been so determined to make alone.

"How do you stand it?" she asked her sister as she shoved to her feet. Keeping her voice down for the kids was a challenge. Sitting calmly a second longer was impossible. "How do you live day in and day out, knowing something like this could happen?"

Angie was staring just over Lissa's shoulder. "I accepted a long time ago that law enforcement, serving and protecting his community, is a huge part of who Tony is. It's part of who I am, too. There are a lot of risks, but if you love someone enough—" her gaze dropped to her lap "—you find a way to live with the fear of what could happen."

Lissa turned. Maggie stood in the doorway. Her NYPD detective hugged her close to his side, but the emotional distance between them still haunted Maggie's lovely eyes. Her friend might never be able to handle the kind of love Angie had described.

Can you?

"I've never been prouder of Tony," Angie continued. "Of the courage it takes to do what he does for this town. I wouldn't trade that for anything, even for a guarantee that he'd be safe doing some other job that he'd hate. Tony's a cop. He's a h-hero." Tears roughened her voice. "And I wouldn't change him for the w-world."

Lissa pulled Angie into her arms as she sat again. Clinging, she caught Maggie's eye.

"I'm sorry to be upsetting everyone," she whispered through her own tears. "I'm just so worried."

"I know." Angie's sniffle caught Callie's attention across the room. "So am I."

"What's wrong?" Lissa's oldest asked as she hurried over. "You said Martin and Uncle Tony were going to be okay."

Lissa widened her hug to include her ultraemotional, ultrasensitive little girl.

"The doctors are doing everything they can." She made certain she sounded like she meant every word as she repeated Angie's empty assurances.

Martin and Tony were going to be just fine.

"Why don't I take the kids to see what they're still serving in the cafeteria?" Maggie's mother offered. Carrinne Rivers had lived the roller-coaster ride of being an officer's wife for nearly a decade. "It might be a while before we hear anything."

With the kids happily sprung from waiting with the adults, the room grew eerily silent. Lissa, Angie and Maggie exchanged worried glances while Matt and Eric looked on.

"They're going to be okay," Lissa repeated as she hugged her sister again. "They're going to be okay."

MATT WAS GIVING the ER staff another five minutes, then he was wading through the hall full of deputies and getting some answers, whether the doctors were ready to speak up or not.

Sheriff Lewis had joined them after Angie and Lissa's kids left. Debriefing the rest of Tony Rivers's team had held him up at the station. He'd immediately motioned Matt over. And after making sure Maggie was okay sitting with her father, Matt had done his best to listen to Lewis's rundown of the aftermath of the sting.

Two of the MS-13s were dead—Javier *and* Joker. Several more of the leaders were in custody. The sweep conducted after the scene was secured had turned up enough drugs and cash and weapons to weaken the gang in their war against their rivals in Pineview.

"Sounds like a good time to try to negotiate a truce," Matt reasoned.

"That's what Reed and I were thinking," the sheriff concurred. "And we were wondering if—"

"Mrs. Rivers?" A harried man wearing blood-stained scrubs rushed into the room, his gaze shifting expectantly between Lissa and Angie.

Beside the women, Captain Rivers was on his feet. Maggie looked like if she tried to stand she'd collapse, so she scooted forward in her chair and waited bravely for the news. The kind of bravery that made Matt sick, because the doctor's expression didn't bode well.

"I'm Chief Rivers's wife." Angie stood, too, holding on to her sister's hand.

"I'm Dr. Hastings. I worked on your husband and the other deputy." He crossed his arms. "Is Deputy Rhodes's family here?"

"His parents are deceased," Lewis said. He left Matt behind to join the group. "I'm his captain."

"Of course." Dr. Lewis nodded in Lewis's direction but kept his focus on Angie. "Your husband took a bullet in his shoulder, ma'am," he explained gently. "There was a good bit of bleeding and some ligament damage, but we have him patched up and stabilized. He's sedated, and we want him here under observation for at least another twenty-four hours to rule out infection. He'll be on antibiotics for several weeks, and I suspect he'll need a good bit of rehabilitation on his left arm. But all in all, we were lucky. A few inches lower, and the bullet would have caught his heart."

"Oh, thank God." Angie wiped at the tears now flooding down her cheeks. "Damn, I never cry," she muttered, "and look at me. I'm a mess."

She turned to hug her brother-in-law, then Maggie, who'd jumped to her feet with a cry of relief. Then they quieted.

Angie looked from her sister's shell-shocked expression back to the doctor, who was waiting with more news that he didn't seem nearly as eager to share.

"What about Martin?" Angie asked. When the doctor hesitated, she pressed. "Deputy Rhodes. How is he?"

Matt moved closer, but Maggie's dad was sitting beside her again, holding her hand, leaving Matt with nothing to do but watch.

"Deputy Rhodes suffered two gunshot wounds to his back," the doctor explained. Maggie flinched, her gaze flying to Lissa, who was staring at the floor.

"He was covering another officer," Lewis added gruffly.

"Tony." Angie rubbed her sister's shoulder.

"We were able to extract one of the bullets, but the other is lodged near his spine." The doctor stalled at Lissa's whimper. Grimaced as she covered her face with both hands. He shifted his attention to Lewis. "Once he's stabilized, a surgeon will go in after the second bullet."

Lissa looked up. Matt barely knew her or the deputy she was agonizing over, and he hadn't gotten the impression they'd been dating for terribly long. But there was no doubt about the woman's feelings for the injured officer.

"What… What aren't you telling us?" she asked.

"I'm afraid specifics about his condition need to wait until we contact his family," the doctor hedged.

"We're trying to locate his relatives." Lewis turned away, bringing his cell phone to his ear, presumably to check whether the station had contacted Rhodes's next of kin.

"Looks like I'm the closest thing Martin's got to family right now." Lissa's chin wobbled as she struggled to her feet. "You're talking about the man I love. I want to see him. I intend to stay with him. And I want to know exactly what's wrong, so I can help him deal with it."

The doctor blinked several times as he weighed her determination against whatever hospital policy he'd have to break to appease her.

All Matt could see was an image of Maggie, standing there instead of her friend, swaying on legs that were barely holding her up, shock and denial crowding out the courageous expression she'd forced so she could get through the inconceivable. This could be Maggie, waiting to hear news about him. Praying that the life she'd taken a chance on with him wasn't about to fall apart.

He caught her watching him stare at Lissa, saw

the tears and the uncertainty she wasn't trying to hide anymore. The shadows of the crippling anxiety she still had to work through—anxiety that the dangers of his job would always trigger.

He turned toward the sound of Lewis talking with someone at the station, finally accepting the truth he'd refused to believe before.

"When Deputy Rhodes came to after we removed the bullet," the doctor finally continued, "he'd lost sensation in his legs. We have no way of knowing if his condition is temporary or permanent until the surgery is performed. The procedure is very delicate. Removing the bullet might improve his chances of regaining the use of his lower limbs, or it might make the condition permanent."

"Oh, my God," Lissa cried.

Matt cursed under his breath.

Only a bastard would keep pushing Maggie to go back to a life where this could happen to her. Yes, counseling would help her deal with the past. Yes, she loved him. But there would always be this.

Maggie wasn't going to be left crying in some waiting room one day, breaking her heart over him. She'd said she wanted out. She'd been saying it for over a month.

It was time he started listening.

MATT HAD TURNED AWAY from her.

One look at her face as she watched Lissa Carter absorb the doctor's devastating news, and he'd finally given up.

"Angie, what if he can't…" Lissa's head turned into her sister's neck.

Angie couldn't seem to find her voice.

"Let the doctors to do their jobs," Maggie's dad reasoned. "Martin's strong. With you by his side, he's going to be even stronger."

Lissa nodded. She breathed deeply, as if forcing her lungs to work, and sniffed back the next wave of tears.

"I want to see him," she announced.

"He's sedated now, while we transport him to ICU." The doctor consulted his watch. "He should be ready for visitors in about a half hour, but it'll have to be family only."

"He has a sister who lives in Atlanta." Sheriff Lewis flipped his cell phone closed. "Someone in my office is trying to reach her."

"I want to see him," Lissa insisted. "Which way is ICU?"

"Ms.—"

"The man's sister couldn't possibly be here in the next few hours," Eric Rivers said over the doctor.

"Are you really telling us you want this man to wake up and hear the kind of news he's facing alone?"

The doctor checked his watch again, then raised his hands in a show of defeat.

"ICU is on the seventh floor." He was already heading for the door, and no doubt the next emergency screaming for his attention. "A nurse will let you know when he's settled. Chief Rivers can have visitors in the ER while he's waiting to be admitted."

"Go see your husband." Lissa shrugged off Angie's touch. "I'll be fine."

"Lissa, I—"

"Go! You, too, Eric. Give Tony a hug for me."

"I'll stay with her," Maggie offered, when neither Angie nor Eric had moved.

Anything was better than eavesdropping on the conversation Matt was now having with Lewis, as he went out of his way to not look at her again.

He got it now. She'd been trying to convince him that they'd never make it. Now that he'd seen her panic once too often, his eyes were finally open to what was in store for him if they gave being together another try.

I don't want to hurt you anymore....

She didn't blame him. She'd love him for the rest of her life, just for being willing to try to make it work. For finding a way to tell her how much he cared, when he'd never been able to before.

Still, a part of her was pissed. Another part just felt sad. As if the future were slipping away, and there was nothing she could do to stop it.

CHAPTER EIGHTEEN

HOW COULD SUCH A LARGE, vibrant force of a man look as small as Martin did in his hospital bed?

Lissa scooted the one chair in the room closer and sat. Maggie was hovering somewhere by the door, but Lissa had eyes only for Martin.

He was so still. The kind of still demanded by the narcotics he'd been pumped full of. He'd be awake soon, the ICU nurse had assured her with a smile and an encouraging pat. As if that would solve everything.

Lord, what did she say when he woke up?

His hand moved, and she quickly covered his fingers with her own. His grip tightened, squeezing in that reassuring way of his. A happy laugh escaped, a watery one, as she rested her head on the mattress beside his arm.

"You…you crawling in here with me?" he mumbled, the back of his fingers stroking the hair that had spilled over them.

Sitting up, she found his eyes still closed, but his heartbreaker smile firmly in place. Then he shifted in the bed, and the smile faded.

"Martin." She gripped at the fingers that were slipping away. Bit her lip against the emotion that welled up when he didn't have the strength to fight her hold. "You're under heavy sedation. It's important that you lie still."

"I..." One final tug freed his hand. He ran hesitant fingers down his side until he reached his hip. "I can't feel my..."

"The doctor says there's a good chance the lack of sensation's only temporary."

It wasn't a bald-faced lie. At the worst, it was a well-intentioned exaggeration. Anyone, especially an athletic, independent, ruthlessly physical man like Martin, was entitled to a few juicy exaggerations to get through something like this.

And Martin was getting through this. She refused to accept anything less.

"What happened?" His voice was that of a stranger's now. Cold and distant, as if he were pulling in on himself. Away from her. His eyes squinted open. "Tony was down, and—"

"Tony's okay." She smoothed her palm up his arm. The heat of his skin, the shifting muscles beneath, were exactly the reassurance *she* needed to keep talking. To help Martin hold on, until the surgery was done and they had more information. "They're admitting him for the night, but it sounds like more of a precaution than anything else. Sheriff Lewis said you went in to cover Tony. If it weren't for you—"

"What happened to *me?*" Martin bit out. His chest was rising and falling at an alarming, too-fast pace. "Why can't I move my legs?"

"You…were shot." She refused to look away. She refused to fall apart.

"Wh-where?"

"In the back." Her voice broke, but she ignored it. "Twice."

Panic flared in his now-alert eyes. Anger and denial. Then he turned his head until he was looking away.

"They'll operate as soon as you're ready." He'd stopped trying to dislodge her grip, but the distance kept growing between them as he stared at the wall. "They have to retrieve one of the bullets they couldn't get out earlier. The doctor was saying you should be good as new after that."

Martin's head whipped back toward her. His eyes narrowed, calling her a liar.

"They're not sure if surgery will fix my legs or not, are they?" he lashed out. "What is the doctor going to say then? 'Sorry, officer, your life is over'?"

"Your life isn't over, Martin. And I—"

"You're what?" he demanded. "You're going to keep coming around then? Getting your kicks sitting by the cripple's bedside and telling him everything's going to be peaches and cream when you don't know dick? Is that what you're looking for in your next man, Lissa? Maybe you could even change my bedpan from time to time!"

"Martin, I know you're upset—"

"Upset!" He let loose a vile curse. "Upset?"

"Just try and rest. You need to heal, so they can take care of your back. Your sister will be here soon, and—"

"Damn it, I don't need my sister. I haven't talked to her since my parents died. And I damn well don't need you holding my hand! I *need* to feel my damn legs."

"I know." He was angry at his injuries, not at her. He was acting just like her girls did when they were hurt, focusing his pain outward so he didn't have to deal with it. A seed of rejection took root all the same. Shoving her bruised feelings aside, she called up the no-nonsense tone that always cut through Callie and Meagan's drama. "But whether you want me here or not, I'm not going anywhere. I'm not leaving you to go through this alone, I don't care how good an excuse you have for wallowing in self-pity."

"Self-pity?" He rewarded her with the kind of hard stare she suspected had backed down any number of criminals. "Damn, woman. A few hours ago, I was pulling your clothes off and trying to drag you into my shower. Now, you're telling me I might never be able to walk on my own again, let alone…anything else. This isn't self-pity, this is the back end of hell. You don't want any part of it. And I'll be damned if I want a woman around whose number-one job is to feel sorry for me. Get the hell out."

"Martin, I love you, and I—"

"You barely know me."

"That's not true. We may not have made love yet, but—"

"No, we haven't. And now we never will."

"But the doctor said—"

"Screw the doctor!" Martin's toneless curse was that of a man giving up.

"Martin, please—"

"Get out." He turned his head away, dismissing her as if she'd never been there. As if she'd only imagined him, just a few hours ago, offering her a place in his heart.

Her throat squeezed shut. Rising from the chair so fast it fell backward, she spun toward the door and burst into the hallway, only to skid to a halt in front of Maggie, who'd clearly heard every word.

"You're not going to let him get away with that crap, are you?" Maggie demanded.

"Martin needs his rest," Lissa sputtered through her shock.

"What a crock of bull." The longer Maggie had waited by the door, hovering until Lissa finally left so Martin wouldn't see her fall apart, the angrier she'd gotten. Angry with her friend's reaction to what was happening, as well as her own. "What he needs is for you to have the guts to keep fighting until he listens to you."

Of course Martin was scared, probably as much for the woman he clearly loved as he was for himself. Of course, he was throwing her out because he thought it was the kindest thing to do. Of course, he was wrong!

Just like Maggie had been wrong to give up—again—on trusting in the future she and Matt deserved. Maybe she'd needed to see someone else doing the same thing to realize just how stupid she'd been, believing that living apart would hurt *less* than the complications that came with being together.

Nothing could be more painful than walking away from what made your heart beat, after you'd thought it never would again.

Lissa grabbed her arm and hustled her down the hall, her tears giving way to fury.

"Keep your voice down!"

"Why?" Maggie refused to whisper like her friend. "So Martin won't know how much he's upsetting you? Or that you love him so much, the thought of not being with him, no matter what might happen, is killing you? What happened to being who you really are, instead of what someone expects you to be, regardless of the mess? Martin expects you to quit, so you are? What kind of bull is that?"

Lissa's shock lasted another five seconds, then her expression dissolved into the kind of agony that had churned inside Maggie when she'd decided that her life would be better without Matt in it, and his without her.

"Oh, my God." Lissa covered her face with her hands and leaned into Maggie's open arms. "I… I don't know how this happened so fast. I don't know how I can love him this much, but I do. I can't lose him this way. I just can't…."

Maggie let her own tears fall, afraid for Lissa and the difficult path she was choosing. Afraid for herself, because her friend was saying the very words that Maggie hadn't known how to say to Matt.

Now there was no running from where her true home was. Where her heart would always be. There was only the fear that she'd given up one time too many.

"Then don't lose him." Squeezing the other woman close one last time, Maggie eased away until Lissa was standing on her own. "Don't let Martin get away with this. Make him understand that you're staying, no matter what."

"He doesn't want me in there, Maggie."

"Bullshi—"

"Stop saying that! You heard him. He's in pain. He doesn't want my help. His sister will be here soon, and—"

"His sister can't give him what you can." Maggie's family had wanted to give her so much, too. They'd tried. But it hadn't been enough. Not without Matt… "She can't love him the way he needs to know you will, no matter how bad things get."

"I don't…" *Take-on-the-world* Lissa was wringing her hands. "He's so angry…."

"You once told me to fight for what I wanted instead of running away." And Maggie had told her to shut up. *Idiot.* "Don't let Martin's fear make this decision for both of you. He can't know what he's saying…what he's giving up. Not right now. You're going to have to want this for him for a while, until you can show him how to believe with you."

Just like Matt had wanted her to heal, a long time before she'd believed she could. And now that she'd finally convinced him that a future together was impossible, she found herself determined to change his mind one last time.

He'd chased her to Oakwood. He'd refused to let her run away.

This time, it was her turn to do the chasing.

"WE COULD REALLY USE YOU, Detective," Sheriff Lewis said to Matt, as Maggie walked back into the waiting room. "I know we may have exchanged a few harsh words, but Captain Rivers has personally vouched for your qualifications as an officer. And my chief thinks very highly of you. I know you've got your own team to get back to in New York, but if you ever want a change of pace and a real fine little town to make a difference in, your expertise would be invaluable to us."

Matt looked from Eric Rivers, who was carefully gauging his reaction, to the man's daughter, whose lethal combination of fragility and strength would forever bring him to his knees. She'd skidded to a stop when she heard Lewis's offer.

Now she was staring at him, her head tilted, as everyone waited for his response.

"You could really make a difference here, son," Lewis continued. "We'll have our hands full pulling together the joint team with Pineview, coordinating the summit between the gang leaders, then working with both groups on the cease-fire that I hope to God we can pull off after tonight. It might not be as exciting as what you're doing up north, but you can help us do things right from the start. And this community would welcome you as one of their own."

What would that be like, really feeling he was making a difference on the job, every day? Belonging to something other than his work, after years of not knowing anything else?

It didn't sound as shocking as it should, the thought of making a place in his life for this town that Maggie clearly still loved. Letting them make space for him. But what would a decision like that do to Maggie? That was the only issue he should let himself focus on.

He'd get by fine in Manhattan, the job would see to that. He was a pro at letting it take over until there was no time or energy to think about anything else. Staying in Oakwood, even if he could get his head around the idea of small-town law enforcement, would put him in the middle of everything Maggie still had to deal with. Her uncle and father were cops. That was bad enough. But he couldn't be here and not be with her for as long as she stayed. And he'd be damned if he'd do that to her.

"How's Deputy Rhodes?" he asked her, not letting his expression soften with the need to hold her in his arms again.

Focus on the half-dead cop upstairs who may never walk again. Maggie deserves better than a life waiting for that to happen to you.

"He's awake." Her chin rose, but she couldn't hide her worry. "Lissa's with him."

"What are the doctors saying?" Sheriff Lewis asked.

"Same as before. That they won't know how extensive or how permanent his paralysis is until after they've operated. Martin's pissed off and in shock. He screamed at Lissa and ordered her out. She marched right back in there once she'd pulled herself together."

"Maybe he's right. Maybe it's better for both of them if she walks away now." Matt blinked when Maggie's eyes narrowed, as if she were prepared to argue the point.

"Lissa'll rally," she insisted. "She'll fight Martin up and down this hospital before she'll let him decide she's not up to loving him through this or anything else."

"That's a nice sentiment." Matt shoved his hands into his pockets. This couldn't be the same woman who'd insisted that their love wasn't enough. "Unless she's fighting for something that's going to hurt more in the long run than if she just bowed out now."

Maggie erased the distance between them with two steps of those endlessly long legs. "Nothing could hurt more than giving up on love."

"Sam, why don't I buy you a cup of coffee, and we'll check in on Tony," Captain Rivers suggested.

Only then did Matt remember he and Maggie were playing out their little melodrama for an audience.

"Huh? Yeah, sure." Lewis snapped out of staring at Matt and Maggie. "Lebretti, the invitation's always open."

"Sorry, Sheriff," Matt didn't look away from the woman he'd sworn never to hurt again. "I'm due back in New York as soon as possible. That's where I belong."

Except going back felt more like giving up than going home now.

Then, don't feel.

Don't think.

Just get this over with, and get the hell out of Maggie's life.

"YEAH, I'M HEADED BACK to Manhattan, too," Maggie said after her father and the sheriff's retreat. "As soon I'm sure Lissa's okay with her girls. I can't leave her without help while she deals with Martin's injuries. But I'll be back in time to check in with NYU before the fall semester."

"Isn't that a little soon?" Matt blinked. "I'm glad you're planning on going back to school, to teaching. But—"

"Don't worry." She stepped closer, until their bodies touched every time one of them breathed. "I'm not going to ask to move back into the apartment. I know that'll never be right for us again."

"Maggie, I…" The tension drained from his body, as if someone had pulled the plug on every argument he'd been about to make. He cupped her shoulders, then ran his fingers through her hair and rested his forehead against hers. "You have to know I'd give anything to have you back. And I'll do everything I can to help you with whatever you need. Including staying here for a few more days until you're sure your friends are going to be okay. And I'll be there for you in the city, if you ever need anyone to talk to. Just don't go back too soon. Not until—"

"Oh, I don't plan on staying." She kissed him softly, then pulled away. "I'm moving back to Oakwood permanently. I'll finish my degree somewhere down here."

"What are you talking about? You've trained for years to work in inner-city schools." His sky-blue eyes clouded with confusion, adding a vulnerable edge that was just the encouragement she needed to see this through.

"All I've ever wanted is to help at-risk kids like Claire and Javier, who could make something remarkable out of their lives if they'd only believed they had a chance." She took a step back. She needed to say this standing on her own. And he had to hear it without the distraction of trying to soothe away the tears already blurring her vision. "I want to make a difference, just like you do."

"So you're bailing on New York, just when you're about to finish your degree?" He reached for her arm, biting back a curse when she edged farther away and wiped at her eyes. "If this is about me being there, I—"

"No, I'm through using you as a shield from what I don't want to face."

"Then why are you leaving the city for good?" He cleared his throat. "I know I'm responsible for—"

"No, you're not. *I'm* responsible. For all the decisions I've made, and for the ones I'm making now. I'm not throwing away anything that's important to me by moving back to Oakwood. I can have everything I need here. I'll miss my parents and my friends, but it'll be worth it. A little hard work, a lot of time, and I'll have everything I need right here."

"What *are* you going to do here?" He sounded almost hurt at being so easily dismissed as something she wouldn't need.

It was all she could do not to take off dancing around the room in victory.

"First, I'm going to tear up the real-estate papers I signed for my great-grandfather's house. Then get busy putting his money to good use, turning the place into a charter school for kids the county's been having trouble helping. One that offers boys and girls like Javier and Claire another option besides giving up."

"You... He had that kind of money?"

"Oliver Wilmington was a wealthy man. There's more than enough money. I spent last weekend poring over financial statements and applications from people who wanted a piece of the trust." She opened her arms to encompass not just the room, but the entire community that had always been the home of her heart. "I never stopped to think about what I wanted, or the difference I could make here. Oakwood can be my fresh start."

"That…that's amazing." He still sounded concerned. "But that's a lot to take on, when—"

"Oh, I'll have all the support I need."

At least she prayed she would.

She'd find a therapist who could help her with the past. And of course she'd have her family, and Lissa, once things settled down with Martin. The idea had come to her on the elevator ride down from ICU, but she'd immediately dismissed it because Matt was headed back to his job in the city. Now he'd been offered a permanent position in local law enforcement, where he could make the kind of difference he thrived on—if he'd just forget about protecting her long enough to take the chance of a lifetime.

"That's great." His smile was bittersweet. "Running a school like that sounds right up your alley."

"Too bad it'll have to wait."

"Not for long. You only have a semester or two to go in grad school, right?" He was pulling away with every word. Making himself accept that he was getting what he'd said he wanted. A life without her.

A life alone, the way he'd lived for far too long.

"Yeah, and I'll have to find a way to intern down here, while I lay the groundwork for the school."

"It'll be a lot of work, but it'll be worth it."

"The hard work's not going to be the problem. My only problem is going to be *you.* I want this chance more than just about anything in the world, but I can't do it—I won't let myself want it—without you." She held her breath and waited, encouraged when he simply stood there, staring. "You and me together, Matt. Nothing else will work. If you think New York is where you need to be, then I'll find a way to stay there. But if a place like Oakwood could work for you—"

"Stop it!" He sucked in a breath. "Give it up. Being with me is the last thing you need."

"That's not your choice to make," she fired back. "Or mine, evidently. I love you. I don't know how to stop loving you, no matter how afraid I am of you ending up like Bill or M-Martin...."

"Maggie?" He sighed at the sound of her voice catching. "Don't do this."

"Don't do what?" She swallowed. Fought against the fear and the memories that still controlled too much. "Don't get healthy? Don't go after what I deserve, what we both deserve, after everything we've been through? I'm just supposed to live the rest of my life the way I've spent the last year and a half, barely getting by, because that's the best I can do and still be safe? Is that what you want?"

"No, of course not." She was in his arms then, and he was holding her like he'd never let go. "I don't want you to be anything but happy, Maggie."

"Then give me what I need." She gazed into his blue eyes and smiled, every shadow fading as she basked in the love shining there. "Give me your heart, and take mine. Promise me you'll be there when I can't do this alone, and that we'll make every day count. We're both survivors. We've made it this far out of sheer determination. But it's time to live, Matt, not just survive."

"Don't you think I want to?" He crushed his lips to hers, silencing whatever she'd been about to say. Words she couldn't remember by the time he ended the kiss and raised his head. "I'll hurt you, Maggie, no matter how hard I try not to. I can't change who I am, and what I need to do. And that means I'll be nothing but heartache for you, every time you worry about what could happen when I'm on the job."

"No," she corrected. "You'll be my heart. Don't let me go through life knowing what we could have been together, only I was too fragile for you to believe we had a future."

"You're the strongest woman I've ever met." He was shaking his head again, but this time in awe. "Are you seriously telling me you could be happy here in Oakwood? That…that you could be happy with a man like me?"

She raised on her tiptoes, until she was looking him square in the eye.

"I know there are no promises," she admitted. "No perfect ever-afters. All I'm sure of is that having you by my side is the only right thing for me. Here, now and forever. Please, give us one more chance."

The tears that filled his eyes terrified her, because she was certain they meant he was giving up for good. Then he crushed her to him so fiercely, she couldn't breathe.

Not that it mattered, because his trembling said he needed her, too.

And it felt like heaven.

"Take a million more chances, baby," he whispered into her hair. "Take whatever you need. It's all been yours, Maggie, from the moment you taught me how to love."

EPILOGUE

"YOU ABOUT READY?" Matt poked his head into their bedroom at the mansion.

Catching Maggie fussing with the conservative collar of the sensible blouse she'd intended to wear beneath an equally conservative suit jacket, he chuckled. He stepped inside and closed the door behind him.

"When in the last few days of craziness did you find the time to buy old-lady teacher clothes?" He was already unbuttoning her blouse.

She slapped his hands away. The backs of his fingers brushed against her breasts. And she might have bought his innocent expression, if he hadn't done it again on his way to tugging the blouse from her skirt.

"Stop that!" She stepped out of reach. "Everyone will be here for breakfast any minute. And my clothes are tasteful, not old-lady. It's my first day. I want to give the right impression."

"It's your first day *running* the school, Maggie." He cuddled her into his arms, the gentle, nurturing gesture grounding her and easing the tight feeling in her chest. "And the kids filing in here in another hour and a half won't care what you're wearing. Neither will the teachers. They're going to care about the state-of-the-art computer lab and the audiovisual equipment for the weekly news and radio show. The library full of priceless first editions, the botany classes in the solarium and the five-car garage they'll be using for shop. Anyone who's more interested in what you're wearing than what you've done with this place in the last year doesn't belong here."

But both of them absolutely did.

It had been a long twelve months, each full of tough transitions and new beginnings. Leaving the city behind had been harder than either one of them expected. Maggie's visits with her local therapist had been even more grueling. But the frequency and strength of her anxiety attacks had diminished, even after Matt officially joined the Oakwood Sheriff's Department six months ago. Medication had helped at first, along with endless hours of talking about what she'd never faced before.

She was still working through the memories.

Maybe she always would be. But she was able to cherish every day now and enjoy her home and life in Oakwood, instead of dreading them. She'd learned that with every milestone she reached, every success she achieved, there were still more to come.

And the biggest success of her life was smiling down at her.

"I do believe you're going to be late for duty, Major Lebretti." He'd taken to both the local uniform and his new job with enthusiasm. He was in his element, wherever he felt he could make a difference. It was an amazing thing to watch. "I know your boss pretty well. I can put in a good word for you."

"I have it on good authority that my chief will be a bit late himself this morning." Matt's hands went to work again on the blouse she'd let her mother talk her into buying for the grand opening of the school. "Now, about getting you into something more comfortable."

"I'm supposed to look in charge, not comfortable." Not that throwing on a pair of jeans and a T-shirt to match what the kids would be wearing didn't sound appealing.

"You're supposed to look like exactly what you are," he countered as he finally managed to separate her from the silk she'd ironed so carefully. "The person responsible for this miracle, the Chairman of the Board of the Wilmington-Rivers Charter School. You're going to look fabulous, no matter what you're wearing. Might as well be relaxed."

And she *was* relaxed, she realized, first-day jitters and all. Thanks to hard work, a lot of faith and the help of everyone who'd supported her, she was finally comfortable in her own skin. Ready to face this crazy dream she and Matt were starting together.

They hadn't talked specifics about things like forever and ever. There was no need. With Matt, she'd rediscovered her strength. With her, he'd learned to trust the love she'd always seen in his heart. They were finally home. Good or bad or totally messed up, being together was everything.

"Better stop lazing around and find something suitable to wear." He kissed her hard, then the hands on her shoulders moved her an arm's length away. "You don't have the luxury of obsessing about your busy day. You've got a passel of folks coming for breakfast."

She'd never tire of having her family over to this enormous place. They would all be there that morning, to mark the school's opening with celebratory waffles.

Her mom and dad were in town, getting up and

dressing in her mom's old room down the hall. Tony and Angie, Garret and Sarah in tow, were already somewhere downstairs. Lissa had promised to stop by on the way to taking her girls to their first day of school. It was amazing of her to make the effort, considering how difficult things still were with Martin. The deputy had regained only partial use of his legs, and he was understandably frustrated with the extended leave he'd been forced to take from the department. Rehab was supposed to be getting him back on his feet, but there'd been little progress, and he lost more interest with each session. Lissa was trying to stay close, trying to help any way she could, even though Martin was seldom grateful.

She'd asked Maggie just last week what she should do. When Lissa admitted she still had feelings for her fallen hero, in spite of everything, the only advice Maggie had was to keep trying. Matt hadn't bailed on her, and in the end, she hadn't been able to give up on their love, either. And look at how far they'd come.

Maggie headed into the walk-in closet, stepping out of her skirt as she tried to find something that was more *her.* Anything to pacify Matt, so they'd make it downstairs before breakfast was over.

"I don't know what to wear." It was stupid to be stressed about making the right impression. The community was behind this school. The families who'd enrolled the twenty middle-school-aged students were ecstatic. And most importantly, *she* was thrilled with the risky adventure she was about to embark on. "You're right, what does it matter what I wear?"

"It doesn't," Matt said from the doorway. His smile melted through the last of the worry that had been riding her since dawn. "Just pick something that won't clash with this."

What was he up to now?

Then she saw the box in his hand. The small velvet box, and the love filling his suddenly-moist eyes.

"I bought this while we were still in Manhattan." He drew her into the bedroom. "But I didn't want to ask…I wanted things to be settled, and for you to be sure…"

"Matt." She covered his hand with hers. His nervousness when he was still the most controlled man she'd ever met, was as dear to her as anything in the box could ever be. "As long as we're together, I'm settled. I'm sure."

"Starting over here with you, with your family… It's so different from the world I thought

I knew. But now, I can't image being anywhere else but. I love you, Maggie Rivers. Marry me? Let me be the man you need me to be, every day for the rest of my life."

He opened the box to reveal a beautiful, platinum-set diamond. All she could do was smile and nod as he plucked the ring from its pillow.

I love you....

When she'd run from him and New York, she didn't think he'd ever be able to say those words. In the last year, he'd whispered them every morning when they woke and every night just before they fell asleep, and whenever they saw each other in between. He still risked so much in his job. But nothing could take away the love she'd finally let herself believe in. The love she wanted to be there to give him back, every day of the future shining from his eyes.

"Marry me?" he asked again, slipping the ring on her finger.

"Yes!" She jumped into his arms as she heard her parents heading down the stairs to breakfast—another couple who'd found a way to hold on to each other, when they shouldn't have had a chance in hell of making anything last.

Years later, she'd look back on this day of new beginnings. She'd remember being surrounded by everyone and everything that was important to her, and not being afraid of losing them. And she'd remember achieving the greatest success of all—having the unconditional trust of a man who'd learned how to love, just for her.

With that in her corner, no challenge would ever be too great again. Not even trying to find the right outfit to wear on the first day of the rest of her life.

"How do jeans and a T-shirt sound?" She glanced up from gawking at her ring.

Matt's smile weakened her knees.

"It sounds just like you," he said. "Absolutely perfect."

* * * * *

Happily ever after is just the beginning...

Turn the page for a sneak preview of
A HEARTBEAT AWAY
by
Eleanor Jones

Special? A prickle ran down my neck and my heart started to beat in my ears. Was today really special?

"Tuck in," he ordered.

I turned my attention to the feast that he had spread out on the ground. Thick, home-cooked-ham sandwiches, sausage rolls fresh from the oven and a huge variety of mouthwatering scones and pastries. Hunger pangs took over, and I closed my eyes and bit into soft homemade bread.

When we were finally finished, I lay back against the bluebells with a groan, clutching my stomach.

Daniel laughed. "Your eyes are bigger than your stomach," he told me.

I leaned across to deliver a punch to his arm,

but he rolled away, and when my fist met fresh air I collapsed in a fit of giggles before relaxing on my back and staring up into the flawless blue sky. We lay like that for quite a while, Daniel and I, side by side in companionable silence, until he stretched out his hand in an arc that encompassed the whole area.

"Don't you think that this is the most beautiful place in the entire world?"

His voice held a passion that echoed my own feelings, and I rose onto my elbow and picked a buttercup to hide the emotion that clogged my throat.

"Roll over onto your back," I urged, prodding him with my forefinger. He obliged with a broad grin, and I reached across to place the yellow flower beneath his chin.

"Now, let us see if you like butter."

When a yellow light shone on the tanned skin below his jaw, I laughed.

"There...you do."

For an instant our eyes met, and I had the strangest sense that I was drowning in those honey-brown depths. The scent of bluebells engulfed me. A roaring filled my ears, and then, unexpectedly, in one smooth movement Daniel rolled me onto my back and plucked a buttercup of his own.

"And do *you* like butter, Lucy McTavish?" he

asked. When he placed the flower against my skin, time stood still.

His long lean body was suspended over mine, pinning me against the grass. Daniel…dear, comfortable, familiar Daniel was suddenly bringing out in me the strangest sensations.

"Do you, Lucy McTavish?" he asked again, his voice low and vibrant.

My eyes flickered toward his, the whisper of a sigh escaped my lips and although a strange lethargy had crept into my limbs, I somehow felt as if all my nerve endings were on fire. He felt it, too—I could see it in his warm brown eyes. And when he lowered his face to mine, it seemed to me the most natural thing in the world.

None of the kisses I had ever experienced could have even begun to prepare me for the feel of Daniel's lips on mine. My entire body floated on a tide of ecstasy that shut out everything but his soft, warm mouth, and I knew that this was what I had been waiting for the whole of my life.

"Oh, Lucy." He pulled away to look into my eyes. "Why haven't we done this before?"

Holding his gaze, I gently touched his cheek, then I curled my fingers through the short thick hair at the base of his skull, overwhelmed by the longing to drown again in the sensations that flooded our bodies. And when his long tanned fingers crept across my tingling skin, I knew I could deny him nothing.

* * * * *

Be sure to look for
A HEARTBEAT AWAY,
available February 27, 2007.

And look, too, for
THE DEPTH OF LOVE
by Margot Early,
the story of a couple who must learn that love comes in many guises—and in the end it's the only thing that counts.

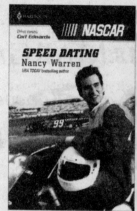

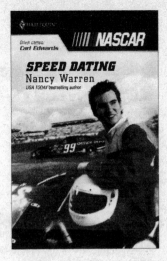

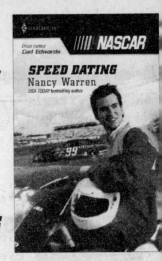

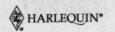

COMING NEXT MONTH

#1404 THE SISTER SWITCH • Pamela Ford
Singles...with Kids
Against Nora Clark's better judgment, she agrees to switch places with her twin. B
the havoc this creates wouldn't be so bad if only her sister's new client was someo
other than Erik Morgan, a doctor at the hospital where she works. Or if her son had
decided Erik would be perfect as his new daddy. Or if Nora could let go of her late
husband and let herself love again.

#1405 FIRST COMES BABY • Janice Kay Johnson
9 Months Later
Laurel Woodall and Caleb Manes aren't going about things the "right way." They'v
been friends since college, but never lovers. Still, when Laurel needs a man to mak
dream for a child come true, Caleb is the one she asks. Will love come later?

#1406 THE LAST COWBOY HERO • Barbara McMahon
Home on the Ranch
For ten years Holly and Ty each thought the other guilty of betrayal. When Ty mov
back home, he discovers Holly is still living right next door. To complicate matters,
someone is sabotaging both ranches. Working together, can they find a spark of the
love that was once so strong?

#1407 TEMPORARY FATHER • Anna Adams
Welcome to Honesty
Honesty, Virginia, is just a rest stop for Aidan Nikolas. He doesn't plan on staying
though he can't deny it has its charms—especially Beth Tully and her son, Eli. But
how can he get involved with Beth when what Eli needs is a man who can become
permanent father?

#1408 A READY-MADE FAMILY • Carrie Alexander
North Country Stories
A ready-made family is just right for Jake Robbin. And when one appears on his
doorstep—in the form of Lia Howard and her three children—he thinks it might be
time to take advantage. But there's something that Lia isn't telling him....

#1409 HOUSEFUL OF STRANGERS • Linda Barrett
Single Father
Take a fifteen-year-old runaway, a widow who's just lost her child, a single dad wit
ten-year-old son and a very wise mother, put them all under the same roof—and wa
a family come to life.

HSRCNM0207